Math Lion Books

Copyright © 2017 by Nick Rock

Cover art © 2017 by Kristi Katie

ISBN: **978-0692865316**

Printed in the USA

Forward

Hello everyone. It's been a little bit since I finished the story, so I thought it would be as good a time as any to sit down and right a forward for this thing. So I'm sitting here in my Pjs enjoying a glass of Jameson (which was a Christmas gift from my awesome cousin Michael Abosamra, who at the time you're reading this should be knee-deep in the joys of fatherhood, congratulations on that by the way) while my beautiful girlfriend Meghan sits across the room enjoying her Elder Scrolls Online. That's just to give you a sort of taste of the life I lead. Point being, I'm nothing special, and I never try to pretend to be. I'm just a guy who works a dead-end job to have a little pocket cash and get through the day, so I can come home and spend the evenings with my amazing better half and our four beautiful babies (cats in case anyone was wondering...not actual babies, actual babies are gross and sticky and I don't care for them much at all). I'm trying to think of what there is to say about this book and I'm drawing a bit of a blank. The fact that this is the story that wound up being the first that I managed to publish presents itself as a bit of an enigma to me. A little while back when I sat down and decided to really get serious about the whole writing thing I wrote down all of the ideas I had ever had in my life. Ideas that I had mapped out completely, outlined from beginning to end and had a full picture of in my head. When I was finished with the list I had roughly two dozen titles. I have, in my life, outlined in their entirety at least two dozen complete novels. Plushie Palace was not on that list anywhere. So where did it come from?

Plushie Palace began as a short story, more of a writing excercise than anything else. See I have a bit of a literary boner for aliteration, I don't know why, I can't explain it, I just always have. So I wrote down the title "Pandemonium at the Plushie Palace" having no idea what exactly it meant. I just thought it sounded cool, so I wrote down the title and merely thought about it for a day or two. What could that mean? What is a Plushie Palace? What Pandemonium could possibly happen at one? I just started a sort of stream of concious narrative after that, not really knowing where I was going with it. The outcome of which is essentially the first chapter of this novella. Not much changed between then and now, a few grammarical corrections, maybe a few bits of foreshadowing, but more or less what you read in the book is how it appears in the notebook that was it's genesis. Once I was done with that I reread it a few times, taking in what it was and what I had attempted to accomplish with it. It was then that I realized there was a lot more going on than just the interrogation of a single puppet offender, there was an entire world here, of which I had just scratched the surface. There was something to this weird little experiment I had forced on myself and I felt compelled to explore it deeper.

There are obviously multiple inspirations for the piece that I would be a damn fool to try and deny. Any artist worth their salt, in any business, stands on the shoulders of giants. Anyone that says they're not is either lying to you, or even worse, to themselves. It took me quite a while to realize exactly how much of an influence the work of Dan Milano was on this story. For the longest time I thought it's closest relation was Meet the Feebles by director Peter Jackson (which is one of my all time favorite films by the way). In fact in the early stages whenever someone asked me about it I would say that it was Meet the Feebles meets Chinatown. Really the world I've attempted to cobble together here owes more to Dan Milano than anyone else. For those unfamiliar with his work (for shame) he is the mad genius behind Greg the Bunny. Greg the Bunny was a cable access show that eventually went to IFC, then to FOX, then back to IFC. He's also done a fair amount of voice over work for the series Robot Chicken on Adult Swim. There are multiple elements of Greg the Bunny and his universe that are apparent throughout this story that I didn't even realize were there until my third or fourth reading of the rough drafts. The use of the word "sock" as a racial slur against puppets, the puppets themselves having ludicrously cartoonish names and probably a half dozen other things that I myself am not aware of to this day. I like to think that Plushie Palace could possibly take place in the same universe as Greg the Bunny. While Decker and Zel are off solving mysteries perhaps Greg and Warren the Ape are having artistic disagreements on the set of Sweet Knuckle

Junction. I want to make it abundantly clear, at no point was I ever attempting to piggy back or rip off any of the wonderful elements of the universe that Milano created, any unintentional references throughout this work were exactly that, unintentional. Now that they're there and I'm aware that they're there, however, it is with a sweet admiration and respect for that world that I have chosen to leave them in. Now perhaps if I had attempted to get this thing published with an established or professional publisher, they might have wanted me to remove these homages and little subconcious love notes, which brings me to the next element of this forward that I would like to address. Self-publishing.

I know, I know; it totally sucks to self-publish and anyone that does it is not *really* a writer...but is that entirely true? I'd like to explain, or perhaps a better word is defend, my choice to fully self publish this work. I know someone who went through a professional publisher for their first book, and that is amazing and I give him nothing but kudos and praise for this. In reading the work though, it didn't feel like *his.* I've known this guy for the better part of two decades and I could pick his writing out blindfolded if I were asked to, and the book that I read didn't really feel like something that would have come from him. It wasn't until later that I learned the publisher had more or less forced certain elements on to him in the final stages. I'm not one to question anyone's integrity and I would never call his into question, but that was something I simply wasn't willing to do. After all, what good is a writer at all if his vision is contorted and changed by the people who are bringing it to the masses? And what are they really offering that you can't get yourself through self-publishing, aside from a bit of street cred and a built in audience? To me that wasn't worth the trade off. I would rather sell a fraction of as many copies and stay true to my initial vision than be forced to crowbar in scenes or elements that did not feel organic just to please some preconceived notion of what my story was *supposed* to be. I'm a firm believer that a writer is just as much an artist as any painter or sculptor; the only difference is that we use words instead of paints and clay. What would have happened if some art dealer looked at Van Gogh's Starry Night and said "It's nice, but wouldn't it work better as a picture of a sunrise?" Don't get me wrong, I am in no way comparing myself to this historical work of art, but the principle behind it is the same.

Alright I'm gonna have to wrap this up soon, going on and on about my justifications is probably getting a little tiresome and I'm hoping you're anxious to get to the story itself. I'll finish this off with a few acknowledgments. I'd like to thank Mark Giamo, Andre Bellinger, Eddie Rock and Danielle Thompson for proof reading the final draft and giving me some much needed feedback. I'd also like to make sure and thank Kristi Katie for her beautiful and amazing cover art (which I was floored by when I first received it). I'd also like to thank my Dad, though he hasn't read the book and I don't know how much he'd appreciate it if he did (it's not really his style), but he's always been unwavering in his support of my writing and I know he's always wanted to see me succeed at the thing I love doing the most, so for that I'm thankful. I decided to forego a dedication as any meaningful dedication I could make may come off as potentially sarcastic or snarky. I considered dedicating it to myself, but that seemed like it might be kind of a smarmy, dick-move so in lieu of an official dedication I'd like to present a more informal one here. I want this story to be dedicated to you, to anyone holding this book right now and preparing to read it, this is truthfully and honestly for you. To anyone who is willing to give this nobody your attention for a while, you're what keep truly creative people going. Hopefully I entertain you with this weird little murder mystery...with puppets. It's strange, it's kinda goofy but also takes itself maybe a little too seriously at times. I hope you all enjoy the trip and hopefully I can keep this new productive trend going and put out more work for anyone who is interested in reading it. Thank you all for taking the time. Truly.

Nick Rock
1/4/2017 10:15PM

PLUSHIE PALACE

NICK ROCK

One is never so dangerous when one has no shame,

than when one has grown too old to blush.

-Marquis De Sade

1

Damn I hate puppets.

I don't trust them. As far as I'm concerned if you don't have a heart you're incapable of feelings, emotions...conscience. A being without a conscience is a dangerous thing. I've never met a puppet with a heart, nothing but fluffed cotton under their spongy chests. In my line of work you see how awful mankind can be to itself, but the most heinous crimes I've seen are committed by damned puppets. It used to be I didn't have to deal with them, I work homicide...homo, homo sapien, the murder of *people*. Then the "Felt Fairness Act" was passed and homicide absorbed puppicide into it's department. Something about how all murder should be treated equally, that by having a seperate department for the killing of a puppet it would somehow be taken less seriously. Maybe they have a point there, I can only speak for myself, but to me burning a puppet is no different than burning a pair of socks...except that socks don't scream as they turn to ash. Looking through the two way mirror at that fuzzy purple perp I couldn't help but wonder, *would it scream when it was tossed into the incinerator?* I let out something between a huff and a laugh. Of course it would, they all did.

"So what do you think Decker?"

Chief Mort had appeared at my right side, I must be slipping, I didn't even notice him walk up. Luckily my nerves are still stoney, so I didn't flinch.

"Pretty open and shut. The perp had the murder weapon on him, plus a bag of muck" my eyes were cold as I stared in at the thing fidgeting in it's seat, "that's our killer alright."

"Well you go in there and get me a confession, but no rough stuff Decker I mean it, he has rights."

"If you say so."

Leaving the chief I had to walk through two sets of doors, almost like an airlock on a space station. The little room between the doors was only about the size of a closet, but I supposed it was necessary to make space for the lining of the puppet interrogation room, some type of mixture of lead and copper. I never understood the science behind it, but the mix did something to the biology in puppets that kept them from performing any special abilities they may or may not have, dampened it somehow. After waiting a moment I walked through the second door and into the specially designed interrogation room. As soon as I did the thing stiffened comically. Everything they do is comical, some people say that they can't help it, that they are just a naturally goofy species. Personally, I don't buy it, it's all one big manipulation technique. They think if they can make you giggle it will engender some sort of sympathy or commraderie. Not me, I've never laughed at a puppet in my life, I sure as shit wasn't gonna start now. I closed the door behind me and walked to the opposite side of the metal table in the center of the room. It started shaking in an exaggerated fashion like some sort of cartoon character in a Chuck Jones picture. It may have thought it was being cute, I thought it was being smug. I refused to look it in it's oversized googly eyes, which were bouncing up and down.

"Got any special abilities or magical qualities I should know about?"

"Nope sir" It's deep, gravelly voice, like nails on a chalk board.

"No funny stuff?"

"Nope sir"

"That's good, that's real good. Although, even if you did we had this interrogation room specially built for your kind. Keeps your uh...talents, in check"

"I don't got nope talents"

For the first time I looked up into it's face, or what passed for a face. This particular puppet was what was known as a "Fuzzy". Fuzzies

2

had hardly any shape to them at all, just amorpheous blobs of fur, like shag carpeting wrapped around a vaguely humanoid shape. It scrunched it's face up into a sour expression, as if it had just smelled rancid garbage. I could tell it was frustrated, squirming in it's seat at the fact that it couldn't make me laugh with it's assortment of theatrics. I smirked a bit, but made it as clear as possible that it was a smirk for me...not for him. I straightened myself and pulled a file folder out from it's hiding place tucked into my right armpit. I opened it and began thumbing through the pictures that were inside. In the movies they always showed crime scene photos in black and white, even in the modern day movies it was a trend that seemed to continue. I can assure you, the real things are very much in color. The deep brownish-red pool of this poor sap's blood popped from each page. He was lying on his right side in front of a dumpster, his arm awkwardly flung out above his head, his eyes half open slits of stillness. As I looked through them I began to shake my head slowly.

"I gotta say, things don't look too good for you my friend. Witnesses place you at the scene, weapon on your person...a big bag of muck"

"Mucks is perfectly legals"

"Yeah well, Congressman Billywinks is looking to change all that, and rightfully so. A dab of muck on your fur and you puppets are three sheets to the wind."

"Billywinks is a joke"

"Really? Now I thought all you guys supported your first puppet politician"

"Billywinks is trying to outlaws our heritages, it's a cultural things"

"It's a dirty street narcotic and nothing more"

I could practically feel Mort stiffen, safely behind his two way mirror. To say muck is controversial is putting it lightly. Puppets have been using muck since the dawn of time in their religious ceremonies. Only now that they've been making waves with their civil rights crusade has it been brought into question. It's addictive qualities are undeniable, just the mention of it sets this thing's teeth on edge.

"Why don't you run me through what happened?"

I took the photos out of the folder that was still in my hands and laid them out one by one on the table in front of it. Each picture a different angle on the same grisly scene that I knew this thing was responsible for

3

commiting. It looked nervous and jittery, but as with all puppets it was hard to tell if it was sincere or if it was all a show, an attempt to make me think it felt anything at all. When I finished laying out the photos I stopped and folded my arms, waiting for it to proceed.

"Welp, I'z walking down that alley and sees the man lying on the ground with bloodies around him. I checks him to sees if he's breathing when I founds the bag of muck. I tooks it, I lefts"

"And the gun?"

"I'z...founds that too"

"So let me get this straight. You found a dead man in an alleyway, you checked him and instead of reporting it to the police you took the muck and just happened to find a gun lying on the ground and took that too?"

"Yup sir"

"No! I'll tell you what happened. You met that poor schmuck to buy that muck off him didn't you?"

"Nope sir"

"Oh sure ya did. Thanks to the new regulations by your favorite politician, buying muck over the counter isn't as affordable as it once was, what with all the added taxes, so you turned to buying it off the streets didn't you? Cheap and dirty stuff that's cut with mayonnaise, but you didn't care, you needed it. Then once you showed up there was a sudden price increase, a few more skittles than you had in your pocket"

"Nuh...nope sir" It was starting to crack.

"You couldn't let him leave with it though, just thinking about that sweet, thick muck matting your fur, tingling the very threads that hold you together...you couldn't let that walk away!"

"No!"

"Oh, what happened to 'Nope sir'? He was gonna take your muck so you shot him, shot him in cold blood, or whatever it is that makes you things live, didn't you? Didn't you!?"

"Yes!" It bellowed deeply from within itself, so loudly that the mirror rattled in it's inset home on the wall. "He's wasn't gonna giving it to me. We had a deal and he brokes it! So I shots him!"

It broke down completely, burying it's face in it's giant paws, it's shoulders rocking up and down. Accompanying this were deep guffaws that were supposed to pass for sobs. Despite it's best attempts I wasn't

4

fooled, no tears came...you need tear ducts to cry. I had hardly noticed that I was hunched over my end of the table, hands pressed so firmly on it's cool surface that my knuckles had gone white. I stood looking down at the thing which was continuing it's obvious immitation of remorse. Something it had doubtlessly picked up from some day-time soap and felt was the appropriate reaction to the current turn of events. I said nothing as I turned and walked towards the door. The thing bellowed and moaned; wiping away tears that weren't there, sniffing up snot that wasn't running out of it's nose. I can only assume it was putting on the bravado performance for whomever it assumed was behind that two way mirror...cause it knew I wasn't buying it's shit. As I opened and walked through the door, leaving it to sit and ponder it's own approaching mortality, I felt nothing for it except contempt.

When I returned to where Mort was standing at the window he was no longer alone. He had been joined by a puppet, a "Plushie". Plushies were the least detestable breed of the species. They were more or less human, except of course for being roughly three feet tall and made of felt. They still lacked any of the blood or organs that made a person a person, so they weren't a whole lot better than the rest of them in my book. It was weaing a nicely tailored navy blue suit with a pink tie. It's green tinted skin complimented the suit in a flattering fashion and he sported a nicely cropped and parted salt and pepper hair cut. To my knowledge puppets weren't prone to the same vision issues as humans so I had to assume that the horn-rimmed glasses that were perched on it's bulbous orange nose were strictly for show.

"Nice work in there detective" It said cordially.

I looked directly at Mort, "Who's the Plushie?"

"Whatever it is that makes you *things* live!?" Mort barked, ignoring my question completely. "and what was all that about muck?"

"I got the confession didn't I?"

"My office in ten Decker, and I mean ten!"

Mort stomped off in his typically boisterous manner. The Plushie however, lingered for a moment analyzing me, sizing me up. It nodded slightly before walking off in the same direction Mort had disappeared, towards his office. I sighed, knowing I hadn't handled the situation how the department would have liked, but there was no denying my results. I turned and gazed back through the window at the Fuzzy who was still in the throes of it's mock sobs. It was quite literally the definition of a monster, yet everyone was concerned with me hurting it's feelings. Sometimes I don't understand what the world has become. We have managed to crawl out from the ceasepool of creation, evolve into the most dominant species on the planet, make profound technological advances that we waste on sharing pictures of our ugly babies and stupid opinions that don't matter on social media and despite all of that, I'm apparently the only one who understands that you need to be a human to have humanity.

...damn I hate puppets.

2

The bustle and clatter of the department's midday activites sobered me a bit after Mort's condemnation. The incessant sounds of phones ringing and computer keys clacking was oddly soothing. By the time I rapped on the chief's door and was beckoned in with a gruff "Come in Decker" my spirits were slightly raised. The small venetian blinds rattled against the window of Mort's door as I entered. They were always drawn closed and when I shut the door behind me we were safely enclosed inside Mort's inner sanctum. Despite ordinances that forbade smoking indoors in federal buildings the office reeked of stale tobacco. It was smaller than one might expect for the Chief of Police of Los Angeles, and the file cabinets lining the walls only added to the sense of claustrophobia. The room was dim, lit only by the natural light filtering through the window located behind where Mort was sitting, which was also covered with beige venetian blinds. Mort was behind his desk chewing on the stump of an unlit cigar, his hulking visage looking even larger stuffed in the cramped space between his desk and the back wall. Across from him were two chairs, one empty and clearly meant for me. The other was occupied by the Plushie I had seen just moments before. His little fabric legs were dangling over the chair's edge, looking like a child sitting at the end of a dock.

"Take a seat Frank"

He called me Frank, the Chief never used first names unless there was serious business at hand. It was with growing unease that I moved around and sat in the open chair.

"What's this about Mort?"

"Listen," he bit down hard on his cigar stub, slurping the liquid that oozed from it. "Your opinion of the puppet community is well known, and while your opinions and prejudices are your own we've been getting...complaints"

"...uh huh"

"That's why, and this comes from the Commissioner and not from me mind you, that we're assigning you a new partner"

The Chief nodded towards the Plushie that was sitting next to me, who then turned to me and gave me what very well could have been a smile. There was a strained silence that hung in the air. I felt something stirring, or more accurately boiling, inside my guts. Thinking about having this *thing* forced onto me by a department I loved, being made to have what was essentially a department *pet* tethered to my heel was infuriating to say the least. Finally the anger welling up reached it's maximum allowable point and I could no longer contain it.

"You're teaming me with a fucking fabric stuffer!?"

The Chief immediately spat his cigar stub at me, as if that was the sole reason he had it in the first place and was waiting for his cue. It smacked my cheek with a moist *thwapping* sound and landed in my lap, dribbling tobacco spit onto my slacks, which I instantly knew would stain.

"That's exactly the kind of shit that's gotten you into this mess in the first place! I'm terribly sorry Jeffrey"

"It's fine sir, this isn't the first time I've been called that"

"Jeffrey!?" I let out in a completely involuntary laugh, "I thought all of you things had goofy cartoon names"

"I find humans appreciate a more familiar name than my puppet one, Zelquist"

"Oh, so really your name should be Tom"

Apparently the "uncle" in front of Tom wasn't necessary because the jab landed home. The Plushie simply stared at me, gauging how to proceed. At least he wasn't dense. Mort looked as though he was about to begin another tirade, hesitating only because he didn't have another cigar stub to launch at me, but before he could the thing responded.

"So if I go with my birth name I'm a goofy puppet, but if I use a traditional human name I'm a sell out...seems a bit unfair, no?"

I glared at it, unable to look past my own hypocrisy which was so skillfully thrown in my face. After a longer beat than I had intended I turned to Mort. It was the first time in a long time that I could remember seeing Mort smile. Truthfully it was more of a condescending sneer, but

I'll give it to him. I opened my mouth to protest further, but Mort raised an outward palm haltingly.

"There's no room for debate here, if you feel that strongly about it you better hand over your badge"

I reached for it too, instinctively my hand shot down to my waist. Stubborn pride is a weakness I recognize, but am not terribly good at controlling. Luckily the rational side of my brain stepped in and took the wheel before my knee jerk reaction caused any irreparable damage. My hand lingered for a second, feeling the cool metal of my badge which had been clipped on the edge of my pants pocket. I chewed my lip a bit as my logic and instinct battled with one another. My instincts, as keen as they were, relented and let my hand pull away from my hip and back into my lap; Mort visibly relaxed. In my anger I hadn't noticed how tense this conversation had made him. Despite his position and his need to reprimand me, I think Mort liked me. I think the idea of losing me over my own intolerances and beurocratic bullshit rubbed him the wrong way.

"I expect good things from you two," he opened a drawer in his desk and grabbed a fresh cigar. He shoved it into his overly moist lips, sucking the end of it, drawing the acrid smoke into his mouth as he lit the far side of it. He held the cigar between his teeth as he spoke again. "There was a pretty nasty killing this morning...down at the Plushie Palace. That work for you?"

Mort's eyes narrowed, staring through me. The Commisioner may have forced this new partner on me, but the assignment was Mort's way of humoring himself. Undoubtedly there was a good old fashion domestic disturbance that had turned deadly, an armed robbery where some poor clerk took one between the eyes, but Mort was sending me there of all places deliberately. Whether this was some sort of fatherly form of taking me to the woodshed or his idea of a cruel joke was impossible to tell. In the end it didn't matter, perhaps the Comissioner had given him an earful about my behavior and this was his idea of payback.

"Puppets, puppets and more puppets...it's my lucky day"

"You get out there and solve me a case!" Mort drew hard on his cigar and gave me a small wink as I rose from my chair.

"Come on Zel, lets hit the bricks"

I turned away from Mort and headed out the door without bothering to look back. It was obvious my new partner was following me by the sound of his tiny doll shoes plopping onto the tile floor and the pitter patter sound they made as he came walking after me. I heard Mort grunt a single laugh before his door slammed in another clatter of plastic blinds.

3

The walk across the parking lot to my car was a short one, despite this however, by the time I reached the driver door I was already sweating. I've heard it said that the heat of Los Angeles summers is something it takes time to get used to, but I've lived here my entire life and it still wears on me. I often think that despite being a Southern California native I was made for cooler climates, somewhere like Colorado or Utah. Not that I'd ever know, I've never even left the state, never had any reason to.

Climbing into the car gave me no relief. As hot as it was outside, the interior of my 1973 Chevy Nova was downright sweltering. *I should have left a window cracked* is a thought I have far too often, which for some reason never seems to sink into the part of my brain that would make it a habit. I closed the door behind me and immediately rolled down the window, trying desperately to expel some of the heat that had been trapped inside, but it was a fruitless attempt. As I leaned my head back and wiped the sweat from my brow with the back of my right hand the passenger door opened and Zel started to climb into his seat. There were cars specially designed for puppets of all sizes, cars for puppets as the driver and the passenger. There was actually a whole line of cars that were specifically targeted towards and designed for mixed puppet and human families. This was a fairly recent development and considered by many to be an extremely progressive move, I wasn't one of them. The idea of a mixed family like that literally made my stomach turn; it wasn't right, wasn't natural. My car was a model that catered solely to human beings. I've never had any puppet friends or aquaintances so I never saw any reason to own anything else. Besides this Nova was my father's and I have loved it every day since it was given to me on my 18th birthday.

After Zel scrambled up into the passenger seat he had to stretch uncomfortably far to grasp the handle and swing the door shut. He scooted back and reached around to grab the seatbelt. It took no little effort for him to pull it down and click the buckle into place. I looked down at him for a long time, taking in how absurd he looked belted into the seat. It looked as though I had won a prize at a dart throwing game on the boardwalk and strapped the oversized toy into the front seat with me as a gag. I must have been staring a little longer than was polite because Zel turned towards me and gave me a questioning look.

"Is something wrong?"

"No, no. You just look...adorable is all"

"Well thank you," Zel said turning his head back around to look out the front window, but was only greeted with the sight of my dashboard. "while your condescention is unnecessary, I appreciate you not laughing at me"

I put the key in the ignition and brought the car to life as I pulled my own seatbelt around me with the other hand. It didn't occur to me that I was probably rubbing Zel's face in the fact that I could do one handed what took most of his strength to do.

"I've never laughed at a puppet"

The car lurched forward and we were off, cruising through the parking lot to the driveway and then out onto the street proper. It was a pretty typical day in the city of angels; bumper to bumper traffic and not a kind soul among them. The Plushie Palace was downtown and it was going to take us a while to get there. I did my best to avoid conversation, though I knew it was inevitable. Luckily, Zel gave me a good ten minutes before attempting to strike up a discussion.

"So a puppets never made you laugh?"

I couldn't help but sigh at this, here we go "No, I've never laughed at a puppet"

"You wanna hear a joke?"

"No I don't want to hear a joke"

"...you need to learn to relax"

I had no response to that. Well truthfully I had several, but none that were very political.

"So listen, do you have any sort of abilities I should know about? I know some of you guys have powers and the last thing I want is my new partner reading my mind or making my head explode or something."

"I do actually...nothing quite that extreme though"

I turned my head slightly so I could see Zel in my peripherals as I drove. Once he saw that he had my attention he reached up under his glasses with one hand and popped his right eye off and with other hand popped off his nose. He then placed them back on his face in the opposite spots where they had come from. He then reached around and grabbed one of his ears, pulling it off as well and sticking it back on his face in an arbitrary location.

"Great, my new partner is a fucking Mr. Potato Head"

"Oh it's not just my head"

With that he reached across to his right hand with his left and pulled it off. He set the now disembodied hand down in his lap and after a second or two it seemed to spring to life. It popped up onto it's fingertips and began scurrying around. It clambered across his lap and onto the center console before leaping up to latch onto my coat sleeve. I recoiled slightly at the thing.

"Jesus!"

It then hopped off of my arm and back down onto the center console. It crawled forward towards the radio and flipped a switch on the far left side. Unknowingly, Zel had powered up my police siren. Accompanying the now deafening whirring sound was a bright alternating red and white glare that began flashing from the floor of the backseat, where I kept the portable dome light. The sound was incredibly loud throughout the car and the light was more than a little distracting. After just a few seconds Zel's hand flipped the switch again powering off the siren, then scuttled back over to it's owner.

"Sorry," Zel began "I thought it was the radio. I didn't think you'd have a siren in your personal vehicle, especially being a detective."

"Department policy. I had to have one installed just in case. I don't think I've ever actually fired the thing up." I reached down and turned a knob that was just to the right of the siren switch. "That's the radio"

I was hoping that turning it on would be enough of an indication that I didn't want to continue our conversation. It seemed to work as we drove the rest of the way in relative silence, save for the songs that drifted through the speakers.

Once we reached the Palace I pulled up front and took one of the open spots. There was already crime scene tape across the front door and there were uniformed officers and forensics geeks bustling around the entrance. I killed the engine and sat there for a moment. Zel reached for the handle and popped the door open.

"Zel"

He stopped and returned to his seated position before looking up at me expectantly. I took a deep breath before turning to him, taking as much of the sass out of my voice as was humanly possible, before proceeding.

"Look, this...this is going to be a transition for me, I've always been a lone cop kinda guy and to have a partner that's a...well, a partner like you...it's gonna be a bit difficult for me. So, if you could bear with me and kinda...let me take the lead on this I'd really appreciate it."

Zel was looking at me thoughtfully before he reached out to grab the door handle and pull it shut again. Zel turned back up to look at me, his face serious, like a tiny stuffed businessman.

"Why do you hate puppets?"

"Excuse me?"

"Why do you hate puppets?"

"Look, see...you're kinda doing the *exact* opposite of what I asked. Could you just not push the issue and not try to play therapist please? Can you just, let me do my thing?"

"I'm sorry Decker, I wasn't trying to play therapist and I appreciate you being direct and relatively respectful towards me. You've got point"

I pulled the keys out of the ignition and without another word climbed out of the car into the equally scorching heat of the day. Slamming the door and pocketing the keys I headed for the front entrance of the Palace, where the chaos of the crime scene was, and I couldn't wait to be in it's insane and calming embrace.

4

The world's oldest profession is illegal in the state of California. Well, it is in regards to humans anyways. Puppet prostitution is not only legal, but alive and well. Puppet brothels are thriving businesses across the country, and The Plushie Palace was considered LA's finest. Humans and puppets alike came here to get their rocks off in a sock. Personally I could never imagine doing something like that...might as well stay home and fuck my childhood teddy bear Mr. Bonkers. If Senator Billywinks and the puppet civil rights movement had any argument that made sense towards their kind being treated less than human, places like this were it. My guess, however, was that places like the Palace lined Billywinks pockets generously to make sure the topic was never brought up publicly.

We walked through the front doors into the low-lit lobby. There were lush purple carpets covering the entire floor and all the furniture was a gaudy and phony polished gold. There were fake plants sitting here and there as well as cheap looking chaneliers hanging from the ceilings. The place looked like the lobby of a hotel and casino from the 1940s.

I stopped in my tracks, my mind went blank except for a single word ringing through my head: *stunning*. The Palace's hostess was a vision, even when she stumbled slightly making her way around the check-in counter to greet us. In fact there was something about this bit of clumsiness that made her even more endearing. She was six feet tall with heels on, with a petite frame despite her height. Her hair, which was held mostly in place with a miniature black top hat, was a curly natural red that reached just past her shoulders. To accompany the top hat she was wearing a red coat and tails giving the illusion of a sexy circus ringmaster. Under the coat she had on only sheer black lace lingerie that did little to cover her ample breasts.

"Sorry boys but we're closed for today" she said, her voice a thick, nasally, New York accent.

My guess is that she was here to turn the customers on before they had to settle for some puppet with make up. A clever ploy and one that probably worked. Even I had to admit that she caused a certain rustling in me. I pulled my badge from the lip of my right pocket and flashed it at her, which elicited a slightly nervous sounding laugh. She didn't seem to be the brightest girl, as it's unlikely any customers would have made it passed the police tape out front, but I suppose when you looked like she did you didn't have to rely on your smarts.

"Oh, right, of course. Head to the elevators, second floor, room 214"

"Did you see anything?" I asked, partly wanting information and partly as an excuse to keep talking with her.

"I don't really think I should say, you should talk to the boss Mr. Grendlewomp"

"...but we're the police, you sort of, ya know...need to tell us if you saw anything"

"I saw the guy run out, that's all. Mr. Grendlewomp will be able to answer any other questions, I really have to get back to work"

I watched her as she walked away, back towards the receptionist desk. She sat down and looked over towards us. When she saw that we were still standing there watching her, she picked up the phone and began having an imaginary conversation. Zel and I stood there a moment as I debated whether to press her, but eventually decided against it. We moved over towards the elevators where she had directed us and pushed the up button. I tried to casually turn my head and catch another glimpse of the girl as we waited for the elevator to arrive, but just before she entered my peripheral vision the elevator beeped loudly and the doors slid open. I jerked my head back around in the most conspicuous way possible and stiffly walked into the waiting lift. I looked down at Zel who was eyeing me.

"...what?"

The doors drifted close, and we were on our way up.

It took less than a minute for us to reach the second floor. The girl telling us which room the murder took place in was probably unnecessary since as soon as the elevator doors opened it was clear. The door to the

16

crime scene hung open and there was a uniformed officer standing just to the side of it, playing sentry. As we approached, the hallway was briefly illuminated with light emanating from the room. No doubt the flash bulb of a camera. It was followed by the familiar mechanical clicking sounds of a polaroid picture being ejected, confirming the suspicion. I nodded to the officer, who nodded back before Zel and I walked inside. The scene that met us was a visceral assault. There were a handful of forensics people milling around, collecting evidence, doing their jobs. They attempted to make sense of the chaos and I didn't envy them one bit. One look at the room made it clear that such a thing would not be an easy task.

The room looked as though The Who had stayed there a week straight and went on nightly benders for the duration. Curtains were pulled askew and shredded, the television was smashed in, the sheets were thrown every which way they could be and the amount of damage to every piece of furniture and the walls themselves was immeasurable. There was so much wanton destruction that one could have easily missed the most important piece of the puzzle, the body. Killing a puppet is much different than killing a man. Humans can be shot, poisoned, drowned, asphyxiated; there is any number of ways to end a human life. In the grand scheme of things we as a species are much more fragile than we like to admit. Killing a puppet can be a much more taxing affair. Given that they have no organs, circulatory system, nervous system or any of the other necessities for every other form of life on the planet, there are only a couple of different ways to make sure a puppet is down for the count. You can burn them which is the most certain way to get the job done and why incendiary rounds are standard issrue for all police officers; or you can completely tear and dismember them into non-existence.

Our killer in this case seems to have taken the latter approach. From where Zel and I were standing just inside the door, we could see most of the body scattered about the room. There were bits of stuffing and fabric covering nearly every square inch of the place. It was hard to tell what bits came from where. There was a button eye here, tufts of cotton there; it was a real hatchet job. Zel put a hand over his own mouth and ran into the bathroom, which was just off to our right. I took a few steps forward until I was standing next to the forensics photographer Candace. She was a middle aged stocky woman with a short crop of dirty blonde hair. She was squatting down to snap another picture when I approached.

"Hey Frank. Who's the Plushie?" She took the photo and then stood straight up next to me.

"That's Zel...my new partner"

Candace could hardly contain her laughter, but she attempted to do so, resulting in a harsh snorting sound. If there was one other person on the force that I knew shared my opinion on the puppet species, it was Candace. She had never been shy about her feelings towards their kind and it made me wonder how long it would take the department to saddle her up with a puppet partner of her own to try and set her straight. Candace was a no nonsense woman and I respected the Hell out of her, more than that, I liked her.

"That's just great, you and a puppet. Never thought I'd see the day"

"I'm not too happy about it myself"

"Is he pretending to lose his lunch in there? I mean...puppets can't throw up right?"

"I dunno, he's one of those assimilated types, trying to be as human as possible or something."

"Yeah right, can't fake a heartbeat"

"Took the words right out of my mouth my dear...so what's the story?"

She sighed hard and looked around the room, geasturing as though it should be self-evident. I nodded, indicating that I got it, then she led me over towards the bed where the majority of the carnage seemed to have taken place. Most of the girl's body was there, spread out across the sheets. I leaned in for a closer look, but could make little of the mess other than the fact that there was a lot of cotton and whoever had done this was a savage, even by my standards.

"Well whoever she was she didn't have a fun time of it. Looks like a pretty typical bed 'n shred job. Found traces of semen on cotton here, here and over there." She pointed across the room to where even more of the victim had been thrown. "Looks like he finished up, then for reasons that are his own at this point, went berzerk and started ripping her limb from limb. Looks like he mostly used his hands, but there are signs of teeth marks as well. Guy was brutally thorough. Whatever the reason, he wanted to make sure this puppet wasn't getting up again."

"Any match on the semen?"

"Well we just got the stuff so not yet, but I'm not counting on it.

You know how it is, if we don't have the DNA on file the most we can tell you is that it's human semen. From the looks of this I'd guess he wont be in the system."

"Why is that?"

"It seems like a first time offender to me. This isn't someone that came in with the intent of hurting this girl. There's too much sloppy viciousness, this is the crime of someone who snapped, abruptly. Maybe I'll be pleasantly surprised and the guy is on file, but I sincerely doubt it. This was some kind of crime of passion, not the work of a professional."

I looked around at the scene, nodding as Candace walked me through her professional opinion of the case. She had damn good instincts and the force was lucky to have someone that was so dedicated and talented. Her hunches were usually accurate and if she wasn't expecting to find a DNA match, neither was I. It looked like it was going to be good old-fashioned police work that brought this scum bag in, and that was just fine with me. My own opinions aside, looking at a massacre like this made me ashamed for my species. Puppets may rub me the wrong way, but no one deserved to go out like this. The cruelty on display was too much, too intimate. I shook my head and ran a hand through my hair. I turned to Candace who was looking up at me, reading me like a book.

"Good work Candace, as always."

"Thanks Frank, we'll bust this creep"

"We'll do our damndest. Can you see that a copy of those photos are left on my desk back at the station? I'm gonna wanna look over them"

"Of course"

I gave her a pat on the back, which felt only slightly awkward, but it's what I would have done to a male co-worker who had done a fine job. I may have my prejudices, but sexism wasn't in my reportoire. I turned away from her and let her get back to her work. As I made my way towards the door Zel reappeared out of the bathroom.

"I didn't think puppets could get sick"

"We can't, but we can get nausous, which if you ask me is even worse. At least you guys get the satisfaction of vomiting, we just dry heave and wait for it to pass."

He glanced back nervously at the scene, then up at me.

"Are we done?"

"Yeah we're done, no need for you to see it up close, it's a mess.

Besides, forensics will pick up any relevant evidence"

    We walked back out into the hallway. I felt the strong urge to reach into my pocket, snag the pack of Crowley 100s that was there and light one up. Having to walk into a scene like that was never easy, leaving one with so little to go on was even worse. Discussing a lifeless corpse so clinically, talking about the last moments of their life as nonchalantly as one might describe a particularly good sandwich was never something that made you feel good about yourself, but it had to be done. We don't rattle. I took a breath and let the desire for a smoke creep back inside my skull, there would be plenty of time for that later, for now I needed to remain focused. Zel kept looking back into the room, then up at me. What he had seen was a lot to take in. I tried to put myself in his place, imagine how I would have reacted if we had walked in on a human woman left in that same condition. I felt a flicker of empathy, but did my best to beat it back down again. Trying to put myself in the shoes of a puppet was beyond ridiculous, my feet were far too large.

    "So what's the next move?"

    "We go talk to the boss man, the guy that runs this...establishment."

5

After a quick stop downstairs to speak with the receptionist again we were directed to the third floor where the administrative offices were held. Another elevator trip and a few moments later we were exiting onto the business level of The Plushie Palace. This floor appeared identical to the second one and all but confirmed this had at one time been a hotel. The only difference being that all of the room doors here had been removed, leaving only open frames. The rooms themselves had all been converted into offices. I absently thought that there were far more offices than a simple bordello would require and obviously there were other businesses at work here as well. Grendlewomp's office was at the end of the hall and the only room on the floor with a door still on its hinges. On it was a shining gold placard that had *Presidential Suite* embossed across it in bold black letters. Obviously Grendlewomp prefered to keep this part of the hotel intact as it gave him a sense of superiority. I knocked on the door, a solid three raps. There was silence inside for a moment, then a soft angelic voice called out to us. It was barely audible through the door and sounded like a child speaking.

"Come in pwease"

We opened the door and walked into what was unquestionably the finest room in the building. When this place had still been a hotel it clearly wasn't the Ritz, but if this had been the only room you'd seen, you would have thought it was. Wall to wall there was ornate gold and royal blue carpeting. The room retained a bedroom off to the right, but dominating the center of what would have been the living room was a beautifully crafted antique desk. I couldn't help chuckling to myself thinking how a glorified pimp's office shamed that of the chief of police. We strode in purposefully...assertively. I imagined I must have looked ridiculous walking so gruff and tough with the cartoonish Zel walking at my side, but I didn't care. I was honed in, steely; a swift and thorough arm of the law. I was in my element.

"Hewwo gentleman, My name is Gwendlewomp, I assume you're here because of the unpweasantness downstairs."

I faltered when that sweet and high pitched voice I had heard at the door came again. It was as if a Gerber baby had developed the ability of speech and was simultaneously drowning in honey, enough to give you adult onset diabetes just by hearing it. As we came to a stop in the center of the room I looked around, but couldn't see the source of the voice.

"Yes, my name is detective Frank Decker and this is my partner detective Zelquist, we'd just like to ask you a few questions"

I looked to Zel, baffled, until the chair behind the desk moved seemingly on its own. From beneath the impressive desk the most obnoxiously adorable puppet I had ever seen came crawling up into the chair's seat. He was a "Beastie", essentially a puppet that shared physical characteristics with an animal. They were my least favorite breed of puppet, the least human. This one was a tiny bear with little white wings sprouting out of it's back. Coupled with giant saucer eyes it looked like a cherub teddy bear. Once it settled into it's seat I couldn't help myself. I bent over, propping my hands on my knees as though I were speaking with a baby and in my best cutsie, condescending voice I addressed the thing.

"Well hey there little fella! Aren't you just the cutest little whore peddler I've ever seen? You run this whole big place all by yourself?"

I turned to Zel with a superior grin on my face, fully expecting him to be glaring at me disapprovingly. Instead he was looking at me utterly confused, as though I had just dropped my pants and started yoddeling while waggling my penis at him. He looked from me to Grendlewomp. I mouthed a "what?" at him, and then his expression changed immediately, his face became intensely serious.

"I'm willing to overlook this little...snafu if you knock it off right now"

I stood straight, something was up and the fact that Zel caught it before me was...humbling.

"Why I have no idea what you're talking about awfficer."
"Can it!"

Grendlewomp looked as grumpy and disgruntled as an adorable

angel teddy bear possibly could. Before I could ask what the Hell was going on I was overtaken by the sudden need to pop my ears, like I had just spent an hour at the bottom of a deep pool. I stuck my pinky in my ear and jostled it around, hoping to remedy the problem which had become quickly intolerable. A few seconds later there was a loud popping sound, like a champagne cork being shot out. I shook my head and then turned my attention back to Grendlewomp and, I'm embarassed to say, nearly stumbled back with shock. Where the tiny bear had just been seated was something else entirely. He looked like a mix of a Beastie and a Fuzzy, unlike anything I'd ever seen before. He had bright blue fur and was large in every sense of the word; his physicality, his presence...his everything. This was a creature that not only demanded respect, but received it instantly. He had hard pink foam for his pectorals and abdomen giving him the illusion of a body builder. His face looked like some sort of badger or weasel with beady ebony eyes set back behind a pointed snout. I turned to Zel who was looking at me, a little more smugly than I would have appreciated, but I supposed I owed him one. When Grendlewomp spoke again, his voice was now incredibly deep and foreboding. The sound was enough to inspire dread in even the bravest person and coupled with his physical appearance, he was damn near horrifying.

"You know, revealing another puppet's abilities to a human is extremely frowned upon in our culture"

"As is using your abilities as an attempt to manipulate officers of the law in their investigation of a murder that happened on your property, sir" Zel said

"I suppose you have a point there, I have nothing to hide. I'm just accustomed to presenting myself a certain way to humans"

"Accustomed to lying you mean" I said, sounding unfortunately lame in comparison to Zel. Both puppets looked at me as though I had just passed unusually loud gas. I gave a small nod, trying not to look detered. The beat of silence went on a bit longer than was comfortable and I meant to break it with a line of questioning, but couldn't seem to get my mouth moving. It was eventually Grendlewomp who spoke and it was the only time I would even silently thank him.

"What exactly can I help you with?"

This snapped me back into full detective mode. I reached into my pocket and pulled out my notepad and a pen to take notes as he spoke. I flipped it open to the first blank page.

"Run us through the series of events, as you remember them." I said, looking towards Zel, for what? His approval?

"Well I was up in my office all day, so I didn't see or hear anything out of the ordinary. It wasn't until Roxy paged my phone here that I knew anything had happened"

"And Roxy is the meet and greet girl downstairs?"

"Why, do you want her?" Grendlewomp asked me. There was a stirring in me that wanted to express that yes, I did want her, very badly. "Sorry, but she's not on the menu. As I'm sure you're aware prostitution of humans is illegal"

I did my best to shake away the image of Roxy and me together, even if she had been available I'd never paid for sex before and didn't plan on starting today, no matter how alluring she may have been.

"We're going to need to talk to her and the rest of the girls on staff"

"I'm sorry but Roxy just left, and I sent the rest of the girls home shortly before you arrived. Obviously they've all had a traumatic day."

"You sent witnesses to a murder home? Away from the scene of the crime before they could give a statement?" Zel said, sounding a little more suspicious than I think he meant to, though I didn't blame him.

"Their friend was just butchered by a client, I had to think of their mental well being"

"Well" I started, taking back the reigns, "We're going to be back tomorrow and we're going to need to speak with them...all of them. But lets get back to the victim. What was her name?"

"Honestly officers, we're not wanting to press charges in this matter"

I was so taken aback by this that I wasn't exactly sure what to say. I looked over at Zel who was beginning to look even more suspicious than he had sounded. He remained silent though and I needed to press on myself.

"Mr. Grendlewomp...this is a *murder* investigation. A federal offense, a felony...you don't get to decide whether to press charges or not. We're not talking about someone slashing your tires, someone died here today"

Grendlewomp's small black eyes bore a hole in me. He barred his fangs slightly before running a black and spongy serpentine tongue across them. He sighed heavily before letting out a small, nervous laugh.

"Of course, I don't know what I was thinking. The girl's name was Bethany"

"Bethany is an odd name for a puppet"

"Well it's a stage name obviously, as for her real name I unfortunately can't help you"

"What do you mean you can't help us?"

"Gentlemen, I work in the adult entertainment business. Our entire industry thrives on men and women that want to erase their past as fully as possible. They want a new identity, one that allows them to...subgegate themselves to the kinds of acts necessary for this kind of vocation. Ninety percent of my staff here are what you would refer to as 'Jane Doe's, I simply give them a chance to make a living while being someone new."

It was now my turn to run my tongue across my teeth. It didn't have nearly the same intimidating effect as Grendlewomp's gesture. I looked to Zel who looked to me with a small sort of shrug, I think we had both resigned that we weren't going to get much more here.

"So you have no records of your employees identities or history"

"I wish I could be of more help. Puppets aren't given the luxury of social security numbers like you humans are, seems the government isn't as interested in the well being of our kind."

I frowned to myself then looked down at my notepad. There was only one word printed there in all capital letters: ROXY. I cleared my throat, slightly embarassed. At least I didn't make the O a little heart. Fawning over some girl instead of focusing on the task at hand was quite unlike myself. I flipped the cover closed and pocketed both it and the pen. I looked up to Grendlewomp and would swear he was grinning, victorious in his deflection.

"Thank you for your time Mr. Grendlewomp, you've been a huge help. We wont take up any more of your time"

I then nodded to Zel and we both turned and began to walk away. I used to watch a lot of television growing up and as one could probably guess one of my favorite programs was Columbo, and why not? He was the best detective in the game and always got his man. He was someone I could respect and admire, and in doing so I had picked up a couple of tricks from him. One of which I was about to deploy here, after having let Grendlewomp think he had won. I reached the door back to the hall and just before grasping the handle, turned back to him.

"There's just one more thing"

I could see Grendlewomp's confidence wane, his smug smile slip from his bestial lips. I was never left dissatisfied by this little trick.

"The client. The one responsible for the murder. Now I'm *sure* that you keep a record of all of your guests for your *own* best interest and I have no doubt that when the lovely Roxy paged you with the message that something terrible had happened the first bit of information she would have surrendered was the guy's name."

Grendlewomp sneered, knowing I had caught him off guard. He had filled himself with false confidence, had come to the conclusion that we were both so incompetent that we wouldn't even question the murderer's identity. It was simple to make him think we were inept, it was what he was hoping for, it's always easier to make someone believe something that they *want* to believe. Grendlewomp knew that I knew he had the information and no form of manipulation or trickery was going to keep me from getting it.

"The guy's name is Alvin Klug. He's a regular around here."

"Any address or other information?"

"Sorry, didn't get a lot of small talk with him as he was...coming and going"

"Any description on the guy?" I continued, ignoring his crass double entendre.

"I would assume a trench coat and a hat...maybe some cum stained jeans to complete the look. I'm the owner of this establishment, I don't often go down to mingle with the perverts...that's what Roxy is for. Now unless there's anything else, I have a lot of work to get back to."

I was pretty sure he knew a lot more than he was saying, but a name was good enough for me. It was certainly better than anything else we had received and to be perfectly frank having a prime suspect's full name after interviewing only one person was much better than most cases go. I smiled genuinely at him as Zel opened the door for me.

"We'll be back bright and early tomorrow, we'll want to speak with the girls you sent home and uh...with Roxy as well, so do me a favor and make sure that they're all here or I'll bust your ass for obstruction"

I said all this cheerily and with a bright smile across my face, which I'm pretty sure just dug into Grendlewomp's pride a little more after having just been bested. I turned and walked out the door into the hallway, Zel followed and closed the door behind us. We began walking back down the hall towards the elevator.

"Columbo?" Zel asked

"That's why he's the best. Now lets see if we can't track down our Mr. Klug"

Plushie Palace

6

It didn't take long for dispatch to find an address for Alvin Klug, as it turns out Klug is not a very common surname and within just a few minutes of putting the call in we were en route to his home. The address we were directed to was about a forty five minute drive, South East of Los Angeles in one of the county's more rural areas near it's outskirts. We drove in silence, which was again only broken by the sounds of the radio, which near the end of the trek became mostly static, at which point I clicked it off.

After traversing some roads that were off the beaten path we came to a long dirt driveway that lead up to the front of the Klug residence. The house's paint was peeling and the structure itself was in dire need of repairs. It looked like it would have been more fitting somewhere in the mid-west as opposed to just outside one of the country's biggest metropolitan cities. I could hear the gravel being kicked out from beneath my tires as we crept to a stop near the end of the drive. As we exited the car and walked to the porch steps that led to the front of the home, I took a moment to enjoy the semi-woodsie surroundings. There were tall trees on either side of the property, though I couldn't have told you the type if a gun was pointed at my head. I was never a boy scout. The summer heat beating down on us was pleasantly juxtaposed with a cool breeze, and the rustling of branches was only overtaken by the sound of crunching dried out weeds under our feet.

Once we reached the base of the steps the screen door opened and a woman I would guess to be in her late fifties walked out onto the wooden porch. She had straight black hair tied back in a ponytail, highlighted by streaks of grey. Her face was sagged and wrinkled, etched with character that only came from living a life that was less than pleasant. Zel and I stopped and looked up at her as she came to a stop at the top step. We stood there in silence a moment, looking at one another. She seemed as though she wasn't accustomed to visitors. I was about to introduce ourselves and begin the unpleasant business of explaining why we were there when she slowly began to nod.

"Take it you're here looking for my husband"

"Are you Mrs. Klug?" I asked, trying to sound delicate

"I am. Well, soon to be the ex-Mrs. Klug if that makes any difference. You the police?"

"We are"

She huffed, then ran a frail hand over her hair. The smile that came across her lips was steeped in bitterness.

"Well whatever it is you think he did, I'll save you some stress and let you know right now...he did it"

"What makes you say that?" Zel asked, taking his share of the questioning in stride.

"He's a sick and angry man...only makes sense that he'd eventually do something sick and angry...something that'll lead to a sick and angry end. Why don't you boys come on up and have a seat on the porch? I have a feeling we have some talking to do."

With this she turned and walked off to her right where there was a folding chair set up. We climbed the steps, each board creaking as we went. At the top we saw there was a bench not far from the cheap plastic folding chair where the woman was now seated. Zel and I walked over and sat down, me taking the seat closest to her. She reached into the pocket of the grimey white cotton robe she was wearing and pulled a pack of cigarettes out. She retrieved one by the filter and held it between her fingers, she looked like an old Hollywood starlet who had fallen out of the limelight. She raised her eyebrows towards us.

"Do you mind?"

"Not at all Mrs. Klug, only if you don't mind if I join you", I smiled producing my own pack of smokes out of the interior of my coat pocket.

"A fellow smoker! Don't see many of us around these days, everyone's so damned health concious"

"We're a *dying* breed", I leaned over, lighter already in hand, and lit her cigarette before lighting my own. She sucked the end, bringing the tip to a hot cherry before expelling it with another dry laugh.

"That's good...one can only hope, right?"

As soon as she said this I knew there was no joking in it. It didn't seem as though she *wanted* to die, just that she didn't care much if she kept living. This moment seemed to encapsulate her entire self to me, define it. The only word I could think to put to that definition, was defeated. It was only a second between her morbid quip and me speaking, but it felt like an eternity. I studied the lines of her face, the distant vacancy in the eyes that seemed to be staring off into some unknown past. I instantly felt sad for her.

"Mrs Klug..."

"Please" she interrupted, "Stop calling me that, my name is Amanda. I'd like to put as much distance between myself and Al as possible if you don't mind"

"Messy divorce?"

"Actually it hasn't been all that bad, mainly because it hasn't really gotten going. Last time I saw Al was four months ago when I threw him out on his ass. Haven't even spoken to the man since. So what did he do?"

I looked over at Zel, who turned away, seeming to be ashamed for Al and embarassed for his wife. I sighed deeply before turning back to her. Amanda watched expectantly, not looking at all worried, she seemed to have already come to terms with what she didn't yet know.

"He is suspected of murdering a prostitute"

I couldn't make eye contact with her as I said the words. Saying them out loud, so plainly, made it real. I was expecting tears, anger, denial; what I wasn't expecting was the sardonic chuckle that escaped her lips and the smirk that accompanied it. She took a long drag off of her cigarette shaking her head slightly before bringing her eyes to mine.

"...she a puppet?"

I was in the middle of taking a drag myself, which was lucky, because that made it much easier to hide my surprise and maintain my poker face. I can't quite explain why it works that way, but it does. Maybe because you have something to do with your hands. I took the cigarette out from between my lips and let out a steady stream.

"What makes you think that?"

31

"I'll take that as a yes. My husband, as I said before is very sick, and he's always had a conflicted relationship with...your kind." On this last bit she leaned past me and pointed her glowing cigarette over at Zel. "I've never had any problem with you guys, live and let live I say, but Al...he was always a little...funny, about puppets"

"Funny how?" Zel asked

"Well, he'd claim to hate your kind and everything about you, but then he'd spend all day locked up in the bedroom looking up puppet porn. You could say it was a love hate relationship. I turned a blind eye to the porn cause, what do I care? If he's doin that he's leavin me alone right? The hatred was a bit harder to ignore, especially when it cost us our daughter. Once I found out about his trips to the Palace I was done. I knew it was just a matter of time before he lost it. He spent a lot of years on that knife's edge of insanity. Someone was going to get cut eventually."

She took a long, deep huff on her cigarette, I was only too happy to do the same. She drifted off again, staring into the horizon, looking like she had forgotten we were there. The sun had gone down just enough to cast a shadow from one of the porch's posts across Amanda's eyes. A single black strip from temple to temple.

"You said it cost you your daughter, what did you mean?"

At the mention of her daughter Amanda's eyes shot immediately across the porch over to one of the larger trees in the front lawn. Hanging from it was a crude swing, nothing more than a water rotted old plank of wood now. Her lips trembled a bit, wanting to smile at the sight and the memories it reawakened, but she couldn't bring herself to do it. She would never smile about her daughter again.

"Heather...Heather Rose was her name. She was one of the kindest people I had ever met, a bit of a wild streak in her, but not a mean bone in her body. She took up with a puppet, started getting pretty serious with him. Neither of us cared for him, but it was for different reasons. Him being a puppet was enough for Al, for me it was the bloodshot eyes and the jittery way he carried himself. If that kid wasn't on Muck, he was sure as Hell on something. Al told her it was him or us, and that was the last time I saw her...pulling out of that driveway" She nodded, off towards where we had driven in, "...never bothering to look back. I should have said something, I should have stopped him...but I didn't. Now that I'm finally rid of him it's too late, I wouldn't even know where to look for her..."

An awkward silence came over all of us as she relived that horrible moment, putting the almost gone cigarette between her lips again. To my left Zel was unreadable, simply taking in the scene. He obviously didn't know what to say or do, so he just let the moment hang there. I took a quick drag off of my own cigarette, letting the smoke out in a pointed sigh that was supposed to say *tell me about it*. I ran a hand across my stubbled face and as graciously as I could pressed forward.

"So you have no idea where your husband might be? No...friend's houses? hotels? anything?"

"Friends?" another laugh as dry as a tumbleweed croaked out, "Al doesn't have any friends. You might want to talk to his our eldest, Colton. He was always closer to his father than with me, he hasn't spoken to me since the split, hasn't wanted to hear my side of it. I'll never be right in his eyes."

She took a final drag letting the filter crack and burn before taking it quickly away from her lips, stubbing it out on the arm of her chair.

"Kinda funny isn't it? I got married and had children so I'd never be alone. Now my husband is gone, in more ways than one, but not before taking both of my children away from me on his way out..."

Her eyes glossed again, it was hard to tell if there were tears welling there at the thought of her shattered life, or if they were just empty. Hollowed out by the shit she had been put through. I hated to push so hard, to not be able to take time to show her sympathy and compassion...but I needed to find this man. Sooner rather than later.

"Where would we be able to find your son?"

It was several moments before she answered, inisisting on finishing whatever inner thought had come to her, before progressing the conversation.

"As I said, I haven't talked to him since the split. Al wont be staying with him, but Colton might know where he's hold up. He works at the auto shop on Fairfax Avenue. If you hurry back into the city you might be able to catch him as they're closing."

I nodded, then stood, taking another long hit off of my smoke. Zel followed suit and jumped from his seat to the wooden floor of the porch. Amanda didn't bother to stand, smiling sadly up at me as I stepped over to her. I wanted to sound sincere, I wanted to somehow make it all better. I didn't know this woman, but at the same time I knew her too well, and my heart hurt for her.

"Thank you for your time and information Amanda, if we find your husband we'll let you know"

She scoffed hard at this, almost as though offended.

"Save the effort. The man I married is gone and it's just as well." She looked as though she finally came to terms with something that she had been struggling with for longer than she'd care to say, "He's dead to me"

We said our goodbyes, I flicked my cigarette into the dirt and stamped it out and just like that we were back in the car headed towards the bustle of the city that was my home. On the ride back I couldn't help but think of Amanda, the beauty she must have had at some point in her life and the poor choices that were made that led to a life of ruin. Of course the poor choices never seem poor at the time, it wasn't until years later when the truth surfaced that their folly became evident. By that time it's usually too late and an entire life is wasted and I couldn't help but wonder how many "Amandas" were out there, heading towards a lonely and unfulfilled end.

7

If I had taken just a second more to express my condolensces to, the soon to be former, Mrs. Klug we would have missed Colton completely. The sun had already hidden itself away behind the city skyline and night was fully upon us. There were some cities that were different at night, more dangerous. One of the things I loved about L.A was that whether it was night or day, December or June, the 1990s or the 2000s, it was always the same; always dangerous.

I parked the car in the near empty lot just as a tall, overweight man locked the front door of the auto shop. The garage shutters were already closed and the lights inside were off, casting the small office beyond the wall sized windows in near darkness. The street lamps that peppered the parking lot were the only candescence granted to us. As we approached I saw him twist the keys in the lock, then remove and pocket them. He turned and took two steps before noticing our approach. He looked at me casually enough, but when he saw Zel his eyes narrowed harshly, I knew that look. He then put his attention solely on me.

"In case you couldn't notice, we're all closed up for the night. You and your uh...*pet* will have to come back tomorrow"

Without saying a word I merely reached down to my hip, pulled out my badge and flashed it at him. He let out a heavy sigh and looked away from it, as though he didn't want to accept it as real. With Amanda a gentle hand was needed, with this guy I could tell that wouldn't be the case. He looked back to me, still doing his best not to acknowledge Zel's presence.

"Look man, I haven't done anything, I'm not holding anything, I don't have any warrants...just because I have tattoos up and down my arms and don't shave doesn't mean I'm some criminal, that's profiling and it's bullshit!"

I hadn't even noticed the tattoos, but now that he mentioned them I don't know how I could have missed them. Maybe it was the dim light of the night, but now they seemed to practically glow off of his skin. Flames and naked half-dismembered women stretched the entire length of his arms and up under the short sleeves of his blue and white pinstriped button up shirt. I'd be willing to bet they didn't stop at his shoulder and spread across most of his torso. I have nothing against tattoos, I actually quite like them, though I don't have any myself. I do think profiling is unfair, but if you want to try to give off the impression of a hard ass then you have to take what comes with that...good and bad.

"We're not here to talk about you, but I don't think I'm going to be doing much talking at all" I said, smiling happily at the shlubby man. "I'd much rather have my partner here take your statement"

I took a half step back indicating that Colton would have the pleasure of dealing directly with Zel as opposed to myself. Zel looked slightly shocked and confused, while Colton still refused to take his eyes off of me. His expression had changed to one of angered resentment.

"I don't talk to his kind"

"Well I'm afraid you don't really have a choice now do you? He is an officer of the law and you'll have to speak to him with the same respect you'd show any cop that requested a chat."

I knew perfectly well that he didn't *have* to say anything. He wasn't being detained or arrested and hadn't done anything wrong. He could simply brush past us without a word and there wouldn't be a blessed thing we could do about it. We may be able to get him on obstruction if we could prove he knew something after the fact, or possibly harboring a fugitive if we found out he had any information on where his dad was hiding. All of that would be damn near impossible to prove in a court of law and it would do all of jack shit for us now. I've learned however, that even though people that look and act like Colton are often hassled by the police, they're too stupid to actually learn the extent of police authority. Part of me believes that they like to get bothered by the cops...makes them feel important. There's really no other excuse for such willful ignorance. He took his small, dull eyes away from mine and pivoted his body towards Zel. He refused to look down at him, but his body language clearly said he would play along.

"Um, ok..." Zel started, "We're looking for your father Alvin Klug. Have you seen him?"

"No sock, I haven't seen him"

"Come on now," I interjected, leaning in ever so slightly "let's try some sirs instead of slurs"

Colton rolled his tongue around in his mouth, disliking the taste all of this was leaving on his palette.

"No sir, I have not seen my dad"

"Do you know where he might be?" Zel continued, "Any idea where we could find him?"

"No sir, I have no idea where you can find him"

"When was the last time you talked to your dad?"

"...yesterday, I think it was yesterday"

"You *think* it was yesterday?"

For the first time Colton actually lowered his face to look at Zel. I can imagine from Zel's perspective, looking up into his round, shadowed mug was rather intimidating. His hair hung down in long greasy black strands. His voice changed a bit and though he said the words "It was yesterday" it sounded a lot more like, *Watch it you fucking sock!*

"Around what time was this?" Zel continued, not a bit disuaded by the hulking man's demeanor.

"It was in the morning, he called to tell me that he would be around the shop later in the afternoon, only he never showed."

"You didn't find that odd? You weren't concerned?"

Colton let out a huff at this, "You don't know my old man, it's pretty typical for him to blow things off. Probably got tweaked out and forgot. He's been doing that a lot more since..."

His words trailed off. He had an expression as though the sentence had continued in his head, but he refused to verbalize it.

"Since your mother threw him out?"

He stared at Zel as though he heard the question, but didn't quite understand it. Gears were turning in his head but not interlocking into each other. That wasn't it, and I knew it. I knew exactly what words he had internalized, to hide from us.

"Since your sister took off with that puppet" I said plainly, knowing I was right.

Zel had a mere second to look at me with surprise before Colton exploded. He went from dense to infuriated with an unsettling speed. He whipped his head around to me, those greasy locks of his looking like soaked spagetti, followed suit.

"Don't talk to me about that whore!"

"Kinda harsh words for your sister" Zel said.

"She aint no sister of mine!" Colton started advancing slowly on Zel, though I didn't think he would actually do anything. Colton was dumb, but he wasn't completely idiotic. This was merely for dramatic effect. "No family of mine would shack up with some dishrag! Doing the things she did. It was bad enough that she left with him but when she started making those videos, publicly flaunting her sin like that. She was doing it to mock us, to shame our family name!"

"Videos?" I cut in.

Colton stopped moving forward, stopped looking at Zel all together. His eyes fluttered and he moved back towards me, as though the word had snapped him out of some rage enduced hypnosis. He remained quiet for a moment, though his mouth opened and closed several times as though he were about to speak. He had let something slip, pulled a family skeleton out of the closet and put it on display...for the cops no less. He shook his head, slowly lowering it as he did. He looked so defeated in that moment, he reminded me of his mother.

"My dad found them, on the online. She started making stag movies with that puppet boyfriend of her's. Turns out he's a regular star in the puppet porn business. I'm guessing that was his plan from the start; lure her into a relationship, get her hooked on drugs...from there it's a short trip to fucking on film to get your fix."

Puppet porn. Much like the bordellos it's a thriving business in our times. Just like any form of porn there are all types of varieties and niches, but a male puppet with a female human was the most popular by a mile. Porn has always catered to the crowd that gets off on the degredation of the young innocent female, puppet porn was no different. It was all oversized foam genitalia and pretty faces splattered with glittery loads. It was enough to make you sick. After this bit of information I didn't almost feel sorry for this man, I truly did.

"They were busy at it too, my dad would find a new one every week or two and send them over to me...disgusting stuff."

"Wait," Zel said, rubbing the bridge of his nose with his hand, "Are you telling me that your dad would send you pornographic videos of own your sister on a weekly basis?"

Colton continued looking down at his shoes, not saying any more, he was beaten into submission and we were the ones holding the clubs. I could feel Zel's eyes turn to me, could see his expression of shock out of the corner of my eye, but my attentions were fixed on Colton. I watched him, knowing the look of pain well.

"You sure you don't know where your dad is held up?"

Colton only nodded. I frowned, knowing it was the truth. I finally turned my gaze to Zel, who was still looking at me unsure of how to proceed.

"Have a good night Mr. Klug. Thank you for talking with us"

With that I merely turned and headed back towards the car. It took Zel a moment to realize that we were actually done, that we weren't pressing him any more than we already had. After a few seconds he started trotting after me.

Plushie Palace

8

Zel was in high energy mode as we drove back to the station. Something about the conversations we had with the Klug clan had kicked off some sort of childlike hyperactivity in him. His words were going a mile a minute. A rapid-fire barrage of thoughts and insights into the sick inner workings of the Klugs that we'd learned of throughout the day. I saw no point in judging them, it wasn't going to get us any closer to our suspect and it was apparent that Zel and I shared different views on what this case was unfolding to be. As he rambled it became clear that Zel was under the impression that the family was destroyed by the father's racism and perversions, which was not a point of view I shared at the moment. When we pulled into the parking lot and I brought my car up alongside his, he was still spewing rhetoric and I had to interrupt him mid-sentence.

"Ok stop!"

Zel shut up and turned to me quizically, unsure what he had done wrong.

"Let me explain something real quick, I was stuck with you because I hate puppets. I think your kind are awful in just about every way conceivable. Don't think that just because we're Tango and Cashing this case that my opinions have changed at all. In fact, if anything, my resolve has grown stronger. You seem to think that this is a case of a family being destroyed by one man's sick psychosis. What *I* see, is another family torn apart by fucking puppets!"

Zel stared at me, his expression unchanging.

"That's what your kind does. You go in, you find a happy human nuclear family and you fuck it up. Something about seeing us humans happy just eats you things up and you feel the need to destroy it. It's inherent in the fiber of your being, if you'll pardon the pun"

41

"Is that what happened with you?"

I was caught off guard, hadn't even noticed I was doing my best to avoid eye contact through my tirade. I turned my gaze to him and he was sitting just as he always was, his eyes scrutinizing me.

"Did a puppet interrupt your family and that's why you hate us?"

I can't properly describe the rage I felt at that question. It had built up inside of me and I wanted nothing more than to pull an Al Klug and shred this pompous little shit to smitherens. I think I was mostly mad because there was nothing I could say back at him, I was mostly mad because he wasn't wrong. I leaned over the seat and popped his door open. I looked down at him.

"I have your address. I'll pick you up at your place in the morning and we'll go to the Palace to interview the girls that were there at the time of the murder...now get the fuck out of my car, sock"

I kept a level tone of voice as I spoke. I didn't yell, I didn't scream and I didn't fly off the handle like I probably should have. He stared at me blankly until I reached that final word, that hate word that had been used against his people for longer than I'd been alive. To hear me calling him that hurt him, I could tell it hurt him deeply and as ashamed as I may be of what I had said, at the time it felt good. It felt good to know that I had hurt him, cause he had hurt me. There is nothing more human than payback, and right now it felt damn good to be human.

Without saying a word Zel unbuckled his belt, climbed down from the car and slammed the door behind him. I was surprised at the amount of strength he was able to put behind it and the interior of the car rang with it's collision. I watched through the passenger window as he got into his own car, some small little two-seater electric number that was specifically designed for puppets. His engine kicked on and he pulled out of the parking lot as aggressively as such a puny vehicle would let him. I took a deep breath and tried to calm myself, a bit surprised to find that I was shaking. My adrenaline had kicked into high gear, I could feel it coursing through me, my nerves all tingling.

I stopped off at a Volstagg burger joint on the way home, grabbed some cheap food and sat in a booth alone while I ate. I looked around the dining area and saw that there was no one else there. It was late, so I suppose there was nothing to be surprised about, but something about the vacancy of the place filled me with an inexplicable feeling of lonliness. I plowed through my burgers as quickly as I could and got out of there.

I opened the door to my single bedroom apartment and walked inside. I tossed my keys into a small tray that sat on the bar that separated the kitchen from the living room, then set my wallet down next to them. I stood there a moment, taking my place in, feeling like I was seeing it for the first time in my life. There was a couch, a TV and a coffee table...and that was it. Moving to the bedroom there was a bed, a dresser with my laptop sitting on top of it and a small fishbowl sitting next to that. That was it. I walked over to the fishbowl to feed Titan, my Beta fish. I liked Betas, which are a kind of Japanese figting fish, because they don't require much care. They can live in mud if there was enough water in the mix. With the day I'd just had I was half expecting him to be floating at the top of the bowl, leaving me completely alone, but he wasn't. He drifted around the middle, his bright maroon fins fanning out giving him glorious color. There's a wonderous element to something so beautiful needing so little to survive that I can't quite describe, but respect deeply.

"Hey pal, long day"

I grabbed the little orange bottle of fish food that was neatly in its place next to his bowl and tapped a few flakes on top, which he ate up eagerly. I set the bottle down and looked over at my laptop. I briefly considered masturbating, something I don't generally do unless I'm feeling particularly depressed, but thought that the odds of me feeling even more alone when I was done was too great of a risk.

After I had changed into sweatpants and a stained white undershirt I meandered back out to the living room and plopped onto the couch. I turned on the TV to some late night comedy show that I only half watched. There were too many thoughts circling my mind to give the dick and fart comedy sketch show my full attention. Then the commercials popped on. The first two were innocuous ads about going back to school and getting your degree in a medical field or some such shit, since most people watching television at this hour are both uneducated and unemployable. The one that came on after that was the kind that was also right at home at this hour of the night, a phone sex ad. This particular phone sex ad was for a puppet line. There was a scantily clad plushie girl lying on a bed, talking on what looked like a cell phone from the 80s. Then the scene switched to a Fuzzy with spiraling yellow and black eyes running its hands all over it's shapeless body, which to me seemed more comical than arousing. The final shot was three puppet girls, one of each type, standing in a line with their hands all over each other.

"Call us now and let us bring your fantasies to life"

Across the bottom of the screen in bold pink letters were the words: HUMAN CALLERS WELCOME.

9

The drive to the Palace after picking up Zel was much more like the earlier drives of the day before, practically silent; but this silence was dripping with a contempt that wasn't in the air previously. Neither one of us said a word, he had just climbed in and we were off, both keeping our eyes firmly planted on the street in front of us. We were retreated into our own minds and it made me wonder what he was thinking, something I don't think I had ever done in regards to a puppet before. I turned slightly on one or two occasions to say something, then thought better of it and didn't. What was I going to say? I had no idea, apologize maybe? For what? After all I was just being straight forward and honest, and never would I have thought a puppet was worthy of me humbling myself before yesterday. We parked in the lot out front and peered through the windshield. It looked as though the Palace was open for business again, continuing on as if there hadn't been a grisly dismemberment on the premises less than twenty-four hours ago. Finally I spoke.

"Listen, let me do the talking in there. I don't know if we'll be able to get anything out of these girls, but at this point I'll take any lead."

"Yeah, wouldn't want me to fuck it up right?"

With that Zel unbuckled his belt and climbed out of the car before I could say anything more. It was the first, and to this day as far as I can remember, the only time I've ever heard Zel curse. I followed suit and climbed out of the car as well.

It was always a bit surreal walking into a crime scene the day after. It all looked the same but there were no cops around, no people crying or cursing God for taking a loved one. It was just another Tuesday at the Palace. We crossed the same ornate carpets to the same elaborately decorated lobby only this time there were a few men pacing around in trenchcoats, waiting for their turn with one of the ladies. They all looked like caricatures of perverts; hats pulled down over large sunglasses, their collars turned up in an attempt to hide as much of their face as possible. As we walked in they obviously sensed we weren't patrons given our lack of shame and gave us a wide berth.

"Detectives!"

We turned towards the registration desk and Roxy came scurrying around the desk. I couldn't help but let me eyes travel down to her breasts bouncing out of her corset as she made her way over to us. Sometimes my testosterone levels disturb me.

"Grendlewomp apologizes for not being able to see you in person today, he's swamped with meetings in his office. We'll set you up in this little room right over here." She led us down the length of the lobby and opened a small door that had been covered in the same wallpaper as the rest of the lobby. One wouldn't know it was there at all except for the small brass knob sticking out. She opened the door for us revealing what looked like a large broom closet with a few folding chair stuck in it. Grendlewomp was obviously trying to make this as difficult and unpleasant of a process as he could legally get away with. "We'll send the girls that were here yesterday in one at a time."

We both walked in and sat in the two chairs closest to the far wall. Roxy was already off fetching the first girl.

There were a total of four girls that had been there at the time of the murder. The first three had no helpful information what so ever. They were either on a different floor or down the hall too far to see or hear anything. They came in, refused to give their real names, wouldn't give any other information about themselves and told us nothing of real value. I was about to tell Roxy not to bother with the last girl when she was being escorted in, but thought what the Hell, we weren't doing anything else productive. She sat down in the chair opposite us and Roxy closed the door behind her.

"You were here at the time of the incident?"

"Yes, I was two rooms down"

I straightened in my seat, two rooms down was something we could work with. Something that might help us.

"What's your name?"

"Cassidy Cane"

"Your real name"

"That is my real name"

Just like the other girls she was hiding behind some stage name she had concocted for herself. That was fine with me, working in an industry such as this I could understand wanting to lose your real self, you'd almost have to. I nodded, calling no attention to her obvious lie.

"Why don't you walk me through what happened."

"Well, I was just lying on the bed in my room, waiting for the next client to come in when I started hearing weird noises from Bethany's room."

"Weird noises?"

"Yeah, I mean, weird noises aren't that uncommon. There was like growling and yelling. I figured it was just another client really getting his money's worth. Then I heard a...a yelp. It was like Bethany had started to scream and then it was cut off"

I thought to myself that it was likely when her head had been ripped in two. That would certainly stop any noises coming from her on a dime.

"I jumped up from the bed and hurried to the door. I opened it a crack and peered out into the hallway and that's when I saw him"

"You saw the killer?" Zel interjected, he was too caught up in the excitement of a break to remember to give me the lead, I couldn't hold it against him.

"Yeah, it was Klug, Al Klug. He's a regular around here, had him a few times myself. He had always been a bit rough but nothing like what I heard coming from Bethany's room. He staggered out looking like he was drunk or high or something...and the look on his face..."

She looked lost for a moment, like she had simply forgot what she was saying. Recalling the killer's expression had shut her down for a few moments, but in a second or two she came back.

"He looked terrified. His eyes were huge, he was shaking, his hair was thrown up in crazy wings. He looked like he'd just had a fist fight with the Devil, and lost. After he looked back in the room through the door he had left open he took off running, down the hall and out of sight."

"You're sure the man you saw was Alvin Klug?"

"I'd testify that in court"

Zel and I shared a glance, if we ever managed to find Klug we'd have him lock stock and barrel. Assuming of course that the statement of a prostitute, a puppet prostitute no less, would hold any water with a jury.

"What happened next?"

"...I went to check on her"

She had seen the body, seen the crime scene. I didn't know anyone had seen it other than the authorities, though I should have assumed. There's always someone that finds the body. I guess I didn't like thinking about that part. No one should have to be that person.

"What happened to her wasn't right. Bethany and I started here the same week, she was a nice girl...she was my friend."

She put her face in her hands and started to sob. I have to admit that I immediately lost any sympathy I had engendered for her. I hated when puppets mimicked human behavior. There was no reason for it other than to manipulate. I suddenly started feeling less confident about the progress we had made in the last five minutes

"Nobody deserves what happened to her..."

I was about to dismiss her, tell her to get out of here and take her dramatics somewhere else...then she looked up at me. She looked up at me and my brain froze in my skull. Every single preconception I'd ever had, every belief I had ever held dear to me in my life was slapped right across the face. Cassidy Cane, the puppet prostitute, looked up at me...and there were tears running down her cheeks.

"Puppet whore or not."

"What the fuck just happened in there!?"

"I don't know"

Zel and I were already out of the Palace. We were walking quickly across the parking lot towards the car. I felt angry, I felt betrayed by the laws of nature; every nerve in my body was going off like church bells and I could literally feel the adrenaline coarsing through me. Any animosity between Zel and myself had melted away instantly, I suppose seeing a miracle on the level of a statue of the virgin mary weeping blood could have that effect on you.

"Have you ever seen anything like that before?"

"I haven't"

"Is this some sort of puppet secret that you've all managed to keep hidden from mankind since...well, since the dawn of mankind!?"

48

"If it is I didn't get the memo. I've watched Schindler's List a half dozen times and haven't even gotten misty eyed"

I couldn't help myself and looked down at Zel with a smile. I don't know if he meant there to be any humor in it, and I didn't quite laugh, but it managed to take the edge off of the insanity of the position we found ourselves in. We were almost to the car and were so caught up in our conversation that neither of us had been watching where we were going. I had such a bad case of tunnel vision that I had already fished the keys out of my pocket and was going to unlock my door before I noticed Roxy was leaning against the hood. Both Zel and I stopped in our tracks and neither of us said a thing. She obviously had something to tell us, so we'd wait and let her tell it. The three of us stood there like that for a moment, all staring, waiting for someone to break the silence. She huffed slightly, miffed that she was the one that was going to have to say something, anything.

"Look, something is going on"

"I'd say that much is obvious"

"I mean, I don't know if Grendlewomp had something to do with that girl's murder, but he definitely knows more than he's telling you."

"Such as?"

"I listened in on a phone call he got today." She held out a slip of paper to me. I took it and opened it to find an address in what looked like the handwriting of a teenage girl, in glitter pen. "That's the motel where Klug is hiding out. I don't know why Grendlewomp is keeping this creep from you, but I'd head over there right now. From the way it sounded he wont be there long"

I looked at the address then over to Zel who shrugged slightly. This was the break we had been looking for, it was in case and point, the only break we had. I looked up to Roxy who was looking nervous and uncomfortable.

"If it wouldn't be considered harassment I'd kiss you right now"

This made her laugh lightly and bite her bottom lip, which sent me over the moon. She looked up at me.

"Maybe I wouldn't mind so much"

"Maybe I'll take you out to dinner sometime, that way I wont seem so cheap"

She seemed taken back by this, something she had sincerely not been expecting. She looked as though she was about to say something more, but there was no time to waste on puppy love.

"You'll be ok here right, you'll be safe?" I asked, gently moving her to one side as I did.

"Ye...yeah, he doesn't know I listened in. I'm gonna hold you to that dinner!"

I flashed my best roguish smile at her, "I hope you do".

I quickly went around and opened my door before dropping down into the driver's seat. I buckled my belt and looked over at Zel who was already buckled in and looking over at me smugly.

"A break in the case and a dinner date with a beautiful woman. Be careful or you might start impressing me"

"Shut up ya Muppet"

I said this with no venom, no mean spirited bitterness and Zel knew it. We both just smiled and took off, both too elated with our progress to remember that only an hour and a half ago we weren't speaking with each other.

10

The motel that Klug was hold up in couldn't have been a sadder, seedier state of affairs. The paint was chipping off of the exterior so much I had to assume it was a deliberate asthetic choice. The sign that read JACK RABBIT MOTEL was missing about five letters and was in such a state of disrepair, I was fairly certain that it was a going to fall over at any moment. If some insect wanted to hide under a rock, this would be the place to do it. It was a three story deal in the shape of an L with all of the rooms facing the parking lot where there were only a couple of cars, none of which matched the description we had of Klug's vehicle. My guess was that after he had realized what he had done he went straight to the motel with the intention of hiding out and surviving as long as possible off the radar. Maybe saving as much change as he could to get the first bus ticket out of town.

We were making our way across the nearly empty lot towards the small manager's office, which was less of an office and more a tomb of bulletproof glass. You can tell the type of neighborhood you're in by how much bulletproof glass they import and I had a feeling that this motel owned stock in the stuff. Just before we reached the teller my phone went off, plucking it from my pocket I saw that Candace was calling me from the office. She probably had forensic results from the autopsy, but they'd have to wait. I clicked the silence button on the side of my phone and repocketed it. Zel had slowed down to wait for me and was looking at me quizzically, I shook my head at him dismissing the call as unimportant. Then we heard a shout from the third floor.

"You did this you BASTARD! I'll kill you!"

Zel and I only looked at each other for a moment before running to the stairs and making our way up as quickly as we could. The stairs were rough concrete and I silently thanked any God that may be up there that they weren't metal, the rattling of which would have given away our approach immediately. I reached the top floor first and peered around the corner to make sure the coast was clear, when I saw that it was I started making my way down the hall, trying to pick out which room the shouts had come from. I didn't need to wonder for long as another shout came issuing from the same voice.

"Then why don't you just kill me already!? PLEASE!"

This man went from wanting to kill someone to begging to *be* killed, what the Hell was going on? The room the shouting was coming from was on the far end of the hall on the opposite leg of the L shaped building from where I was standing. The door was open and I could see what appeared to be a puppet standing in the doorway with a gun in his hand, aiming it into the darkness of the room. I pulled my gun and leveled it at him from across the railing.

"Freeze! Los Angeles Police Department! Drop your weapon now!"

The puppet turned to my yelling and I got a better look at him. He was a Plushie with yellow colored skin and slicked back black plastic hair. His arms were covered with cross-stitch tattoos and he looked like he had been hitting the muck hard. He saw me with the gun aimed at him and muttered a curse to himself. He turned back to look into the room and without hesitating fired a shot through the doorway. I did the only thing I could think to do and fired my own shot. My bullet hit it's mark and tore half of the right side of the puppet's head open. Cotton fluff flew out and fluttered delicately to the floor. The puppet, being hit, rushed into the safety of the room. I instantly broke into a sprint.

I reached the room only a few seconds later and was surprised that Zel had managed to keep pace with me and arrived at my side immediately. I had only a split second to assess the room and what needed to happen. There was a man lying on the bed bleeding badly from his guts. Though I had never seen a picture or even gotten a very detailed description of him, I knew immediately that the man was Klug. I looked up to the wall opposite me and saw the yellow puppet, now with his head half shot off, standing on the sill of the open window.

"Freeze! Don't..."

Before I could even finish the command the puppet flung himself from the window, which would deposit him on the backside of the motel three stories below us. I suppose it would be worth mentioning now, puppets are essentially immune to falling great distances. With no bones to break or organs to be punctured they could jump off the edge of the Grand fucking Canyon and get up and walk away just fine. I turned to Zel, knowing that he shared this specific gift of biology.

"Go after him! I'll tend to Klug"

I walked over the bed, holstering my weapon as I did. Klug was lying on his side putting as much pressure on his stomach as he could, attempting to stem the flow of blood and failing miserably. Zel hurried over the window, but stopped, looking out into the lot.

"What are you waiting for!?"

"He's gone Decker. There was a black, plateless sedan waiting for him. They're history. Why weren't you firing your incendiary rounds?"

"I don't even have them on me, I thought if we were doing any shooting it was going to be at this asshole"

I pulled out my phone and saw that Candace was calling me again, I quickly denied the call and made my own call to get an ambulance there. I hung up before waiting for a response, they'd be on their way as soon as the call was made anyways. I repocketed the phone again and hunkered down next to the bed to get to eye level with Klug.

"You're gonna be alright Klug, the ambulance is on the way."

Klug was a very unpleasant looking man. Just over the hill of middle age, thinning curly black hair that stuck out on all sides, except on top where there was none at all. He had a five o'clock shadow and sunken in eyes looking like he had experienced a lifetime of drug use. Nothing as esoteric as muck either, my guess would be crystal meth or crack cocaine...or both. To say he looked unkempt would be putting it mildly. He turned his weathered and badly pock marked face to mine and spat directly in my eye.

"Fuck you and fuck your ambulence. Just let me die...I deserve it"

"For what?" I asked, wiping the spit off with the edge of my hand, "killing the prostitute?"

With surprising vigor for someone who currently had a bullet in his belly Klug made to lunge at me. Moving his hands caused the blood to flow even worse, he quickly thought better of it and put his hands back over the hole.

"Don't you dare talk about her like that! I'll rip your fucking eyes out!"

"Quite defensive over some whore you bedded and shredded"

"SHE WASN'T A WHORE! SHE WAS MY DAUGHTER!"

11

If there's one thing I hate more than puppets, it's vending machine coffee. Unfortunately for me that was all the hospital cafeteria was offering and as the old saying goes, any shelter in a storm. I stood watching as the thick and nearly black fluid, that resembled crude oil more than actual coffee, violently spat down into the styrofoam cup I dutifully held in place underneath. The entire time I looked sadly down at this display, wishing that there was a coffee shop within walking distance...anything other than this. Zel had been rambling endlessly at my back. He had devolved back into his overactive hyper-speak ever since the ambulance arrived and loaded Klug into the back of it. He was just coming out of surgery now. The doctors said he'd be fine but it would be a little bit before he'd be able to talk to us.

As soon as the rattling thing finished it's machinations I lifted the cup up and took a long swallow, not bothering to blow on it or add any of the modern day luxuries like sugar and cream. I turned to Zel who was still mid ramble.

"Stop!" I nearly shouted, and thankfully he did. "Lets just sit down for a minute alright?"

We walked over to one of the empty tables and each took a seat, I was savoring the relative silence for as long as I could, knowing as soon as I gave Zel the go ahead he would launch right back into a new speech.

"I look at this two ways" I began, hoping to stop the flow of babble before it had a chance to start up again. "Either Klug is insane and he slaughtered that poor girl in an act of aggressive transference, channeling the guilt he had been harboring for destroying his family. Or, *we're* insane for even humoring the thought that what he claimed was the truth. There is no way that a just and loving God would allow what he's saying to *be*

55

true"

Zel sat in silence for a moment, looking down at the top of the table, perhaps getting lost in it's speckled blue and grey pattern.

"You don't think it's even possible? I thought a good cop always looked at things from all angles"

"A good cop always looks at things *rationally,* there is no rationality behind listening to the outbursts of a drug-addled, psychotic killer"

"What about the crying girl at the Palace?"

I refused to acknowledge that and stared into my coffee.

I took another long drink of the sludge and in spite of myself, was disappointed when I finished the last of it.

The doors to the cafeteria flung open with a force that was hard to ignore. Whoever was coming in wanted to make their presence known and I shouldn't have been surprised when that person turned out to be Candace.

"Shit" I muttered to myself. I looked down at my phone and saw I had three more missed calls from her. Why was I ignoring her? *Cause now you know what she has to say, and you don't want to hear it.* She was looking around the room for us and when we were finally spotted she came marching over, clearly fueled by the irish piss and vinegar that ran through her veins. She was about fifteen feet away when she started in on us at the top of her voice.

"Can no one answer a fucking phone call in this day and age?"

I turned to the table next to us and saw a sad little girl sitting there with her equally sad looking father. They were holding each other's hands across the top of the table. The girl was now looking up at Candace, visibly shaken by the monster of a woman that had stormed the cafeteria like it was Normandy. The father had only a look of indignation.

"Wanna curb the language hon?" I nodded towards the little girl

"Oh fuck her! And don't 'hon' me Frank, don't 'hon' me, alright!? I've been calling you all morning and you damn well know that what I have to say is important or I wouldn't be blowing up your cell phone!"

I half expected the father to rise to his daughter's defence at the unprovoked vulgarity launched at her. He seemed a bit too smart for that though and let it go, not wanting to incur the wrath that was now directly aimed at me. I gave him an apologetic frown and he nodded ever so slightly. I turned back to Candace who was still glowering over me expectantly.

"So what's the emergency then?"

Immediately her demeanor changed, like I had just pulled her pants down in front of everyone. She softened and for the first time in all the years I had known her, she looked weak.

"Not here...somewhere private. Where people can't hear"

I had a feeling I already knew what was coming. Candace has never been known for her discretion and her wanting to speak privately was a sign that she was going to drop a bomb on us; like she had just found evidence that the government was in on the 9/11 attacks or that she finally knew the identity of JFK's *real* killer. I sighed heavily, standing and preparing to walk into the information I had just been trying to deny to Zel for the past two hours. Zel also began to get up and the fire returned to Candace's cheeks.

"Not the sock! Just you, I don't want his kind anywhere near me."

Zel faltered, but I geastured for him to stand.

"It's alright Candace, if you're going to tell me what I think you're going to tell me, this guy will be your best friend in keeping me from sending you both to the loony bin"

She eyed Zel suspiciously. I thought she was going to continue to fight it, but she relented and started off ahead of us, out of the cafeteria. We followed her through the double doors towards a more private setting.

As soon as I had flipped the lock on the inside of the men's room door, Candace launched into another full on assault, this one however was physical as opposed to her typical verbal attacks. She slapped and punched my arms and upper body as I instinctually cowered away from her. Her attacks came one on top of the other, half hearted, but still painful.

"What's wrong with you, you fuckin' ass!?"

She finally stopped hitting me and I was able to lower my guard slightly, which was unfortunate because I couldn't help but laugh a little at her outburst. She raised her fists again.

"You think this is funny!?"

"No, no I don't Candace"

"When have I ever called you a dozen times in a morning like that? When have I ever hunted you down like this? Did it pass through your stupid mind that I might have something of a little gravity to tell you?"

"It did I just...wasn't ready to hear it"

Candace lowered her fists again and looked at me with something like confused sadness in her eyes, as though the wind had been taken out of her sails.

"Why are you acting like you already know?"

"Cause I think we do" Zel interjected, "There was human DNA in that puppet that was killed, wasn't there?"

Candace turned to him, for the first time with no anger or hatred, just the same befuddlement she had been directing at me. She started to speak to him, then seemed to catch herself associating with one of *them* and turned back to me. Her mouth was opening and closing but no words were coming out.

"So it's true?" I asked

"Well...to put it simply yes. It appears that there were veins and blood and an entire circulatory system that aren't found in puppets. They were only faint traces, could only be seen under a microscope, it was as if they were in the process of fading away, like it was being absorbed *into* the fabric. I imagine a little bit longer and there wouldn't have been any sign of them what so ever."

Zel and I exchanged a quick look. I was expecting him to be wearing an *I told you so* expression, but he wasn't. He simply looked grim and concerned, taking in the seriousness of the situation and it's implications.

"But how do you know all this already?"

"There was an incident with one of the girls at the Palace and now Klug is claiming the girl that he murdered was his own daughter...it's starting to look like he might be right"

The color left Candace's face in record time, in a mere second her face was the sort of pale green that was usually a precursor to vomiting your guts up. She was a tough woman and seeing her lose her nerve like that was...unsettling.

"Who knows about this?" Zel asked, breaking the silence.

"Just me so far, but that's only because I can't decide which news outlet to go to first"

"You can't tell anyone about this. None of us can" I turned away from her after saying it, not being able to face the criticism that I was sure would follow. I put my hands flat on the sink, which I remember briefly thinking was oddly dirty for a hospital. The same with the mirror I gazed up into, finding my face, something that was real. I've always found the mind's ability to distract itself with mundane minutae when it doesn't want to commit to grappling with existential crisis fascinating. Though I was only staring into my own eyes in the reflection, attempting to anchor myself, I could see behind me that Candace was back to opening and closing her mouth uselessly. She was near the point of explosion and I needed to somehow make her understand. I shifted my eyes from my own to her's in the mirror, still not speaking directly to her.

"Candy, do you have any idea what would happen if this information got out? Do you have *any* idea?"

"He's right. If this got out there would be rioting, acts of racially charged violence in record numbers. It would set my people's civil rights movement back a thousand years"

"Maybe it should!" Candace roared, now turning her rage on Zel. "Your species have been somehow changing mine into monsters! Why shouldn't there be acts of violence against you? There should be a goddamn civil war against you things!"

"You've proven my point exactly. You're talking about full on war with puppets, and I'm sure that you aren't the only one who would jump on the bandwagon. Is that what we really want? Is that what this world needs? We don't even know how big this thing is. Is it just Grendlewomp and his seedy organization or is it bigger than that? We can't let this information out and start a full blown race war if it's just one scumbag, can we?"

I had been studying Candace's reflection in the mirror as I spoke, though she still visibly had her edge, it seemed as though reason had started to dull it. She knew what I was saying was right despite her own prejudices. I took one last look at myself coupled with a deep breath, then righted myself and turned back towards Candace and Zel. No longer looking at them through the grimey filter of a bathroom mirror, the heavy realness of the situation set in. The three of us, standing in this room, had the ability to change the face of the world if we chose to. To send one species after another with torches and pitchforks, likely ending in genocide.

"I don't know how long I can keep this under wraps" Candace began, "They're going to need my report eventually and if I'm going to skew facts it'll need to be soon. If this is big, if this goes beyond Grendle-whatever I'll start screaming this shit from the rooftops."

"And I wouldn't blame you." Zel had been leaning into a corner where the wall met the hard blue plastic handicapped stall. He pushed himself away and stepped forward as he spoke. "If this *is* some...conspiracy, I want to know as much as you do...and I'd think it's just as wrong as you do. Whichever it winds up being, it needs to be stopped."

I was about to argue, I was about to say that as soon as I took Klug's statement I was done. I'm a homicide cop, I have no interest in espionage or uncovering global secrets. I'll leave that to the Fox Mulders of the world. Just before I could explain this, there was a banging on the door. I unlocked it expecting to tell some person that this bathroom had been comendeered when I saw the doctor we had spoken to upon arriving. He peered through the open door, assesing who was there and what was going on. He turned back to me.

"Someone had said you guys came in here...Klug's awake."

I chewed my lip a moment and told him we'd be right out before closing the door. I gave Zel a nod and he stepped past Candace over to me getting ready to go to work. I opened the door for him and he walked out. Before I left the bathroom I looked back at Candace who was completely expressionless, something I don't think I'd ever seen from her. I couldn't blame her, what we were discussing was so bizarre and unprecedented, and for it to carry so much importance...it was stupifying.

"Just...sit on this for as long as you can, let Zel and me see if we can't figure something out."

"You trust him?"

I chuckled almost immediately, partly at the audacity of the question and partly at the fact that just yesterday I wouldn't have found it audacious at all. Now I did.

"Yeah...yeah I do actually. Can you believe it?"

"Not really, no. I hope it's not misplaced Frank"

"It's not"

12

I felt a hint of nausea as I opened the door and walked into Alvin Klug's room. I've never liked hospitals. Ever since I watched my father waste away in front of my eyes, withered and ruined by lung cancer, I've found them nearly intolerable. In the cafeteria or the lobby it's easy to pretend I'm in a high school or an office building, but in these rooms there was no hiding the fact; these are the rooms where people came to die.

I strode in with Zel close behind me. I did my best to put on a steel mask, in case my face decided to betray me and expose my anxiety. As I entered I looked across the room and saw Klug sitting up in his bed. He had tubes going into his nose and arms, much like my father had when I watched the light leave his eyes. I feigned a smile, perhaps over compensating, and when I spoke my voice was full of mirth and good cheer.

"Hey Klug, how's the gut?"

He took a look at both of us coming in and shifted under his stiff hospital sheets, wearing a glower that was hard to define. His eyebrows were brought down in a furrow and his lips were slightly pursed giving him the illusion of an oversized pouting toddler.

"I suppose you're here for a thank you for saving my life"

"I can't think of a person alive who would thank us for such a service"

At this his expression softened a bit, as though the fact that he was universally disliked was something he had always known, but never wanted to admit to himself before.

"Maybe you're right about that...so what do you want?"

I grabbed a couple of the visitors chairs that were sitting against the wall opposite the foot of Klug's bed and set them down to his right side. I took the seat closest to the head of Klug's bed while Zel hopped into the other. I didn't like being as close to the man as I was. He had a toxic energy to him, but there were certain things that had to be tolerated in the name of the job.

"What do you *think* we're here for? We need to know what happened."

"I already told you what happened, the puppet was my daughter and I shredded her, that guy shot me, what more do you need?"

"Well, knowing why you're under the impression that puppet was your daughter would be a great start" Zel interjected, "Maybe you just walk us through it, from the beginning"

Klug eyed us both, then reached over and grabbed a glass of room temperature water that had been sitting on the small swivel table that was attached to the head of his bed. He swallowed a mouthful of it with no small effort. Some of it dribbled down his chin and he wiped it away before starting.

"I went to the Palace, like I tend to do...either of you boys ever go to the Palace?"

We shook our heads

"You're missing out. Those puppets may be God's biggest mistake, but they sure know how to milk a shaft, let me tell you. Anyways I showed up and took a look at the menu. I saw there was a girl I hadn't tried yet and I told Roxy that was the one I wanted...only because I couldn't have *her* of course."

Rage flashed up inside of me, from somewhere deep in my chest and I felt it's heat fill my face, "Why don't you just stick to the story"

"Right" he said, seeming to sense that he had made a verbal misstep, "I go upstairs to meet the girl right? I walk in and everything goes great. It makes me sick to think about now, knowing what I know...but she was the best fuck I've ever had. She did things I've only seen in videos."

"Like the videos she was making before her supposed transformation?"

There was no reason for me to interject with that particular dig, I just felt good doing it. Maybe it was cause Klug was such a rancid piece of shit. Maybe it was because of what he had said about Roxy. I was expecting him to flip out. For him to start yelling and screaming, cause that seemed to be Al's go to move for just about every human interaction,

62

but he didn't. Maybe he was past all that, maybe he was done with it. He just gave me a look, thought about it, then nodded a little.

"Yeah, just like those actually...maybe if I had been paying attention I would have realized it was some of the same stuff. The same moves...anyways, I'm on top of her pounding away and I blast my batch up inside her, right? I stayed there a minute, catching my breath, but then as I started to push myself up and pull out of her...I look down at her face..."

Klug's eyes went dull, it reminded me of the look his wife Amanda had so many times during our talk about this lump of shit sitting in front of us. Reading him in that moment was, and to this day still is, one of the most difficult moments I have had in my career in law enforcement. He looked sad as though he was about to cry, but there was something else there too, a longing or a...lustful haze. He was ashamed of what he had done, but in that moment, looking at his face...I knew he had enjoyed it and given another opportunity, even knowing the truth, he wouldn't hesitate in doing it again.

"Tears were rolling down her cheeks. I've never seen a puppet cry in my life, I didn't think puppets were capable of it...didn't know they had the right equipment. It was then, knowing that, looking into her sewn on button eyes, seeing myself reflected in them, gazing back up at me that I knew...this wasn't just some puppet whore, this was my daughter, this was my Heather. I saw the recognition in her eyes too, it must have hit her a little sooner than me. That's why she was crying and why she wasn't too in shock to say what she said."

"What was that?"

"She said....dad, but as like, a question, ya know? She needed me to confirm to her that I was who she was now realizing I was. Like she had just remembered she had a dad to begin with, like she was waking up from a dream. That was when I lost it. Knowing what I had done and that I would have to live with that. Thinking of her trying to live with the knowledge of the things she had done to her own father...it would have been inhumane *not* to kill her. I did the only thing I could think to do..."

He stopped there, didn't go into the details, didn't need to. We had seen his handywork. We knew what he had done and how viciously and thoroughly he had done it. I tried to unknow the information that Candace had told us, tried to think of how I would have proceeded not knowing that the insane story this man had told was probably the truth.

"So that's what made you think she was your daughter? A gut instinct and a prostitute calling you daddy? Or at least that's what you claim, for all we know she didn't say anything. For all we know she called you out for being the sad fat pervert you are and you lost your mind, tore her up in some self-righteous rage"

"I'm no pervert, there's nothing wrong with me"

"Going to whore houses, spending all day and night locked up in your room watching demented pornography, sending your own son videos of your his own sister doing God knows what...yeah, that sounds perfectly normal"

Klug stared daggers through me, his eyes spitting the venom that his mouth wasn't able to articulate into words due to the shock of having his sins thrown in his face. At that moment I flashed on what Amanda had said about her husband, *he's a sick and angry man*. I didn't understand that as well as I did now, looking into his eyes.

"You spoke with my family?"

"All the ones you haven't allegedly killed, yeah. That's how I knew about the videos. They seem to paint a very specific picture of you and the one word that keeps flashing in big bright letters is pervert"

"I'm no pervert! Now I admit, I've seen a lot of things in my day. I've seen a woman's breasts nailed to a plank of wood. I've seen a woman fit and entire two-liter bottle of soda up her asshole. I have seen a woman swallow a gallon of cum and ask for seconds."

"You're not making a terribly strong argument. You're listing those things like they're some sort of *accomplishments*."

"Some people have an encyclopedic knowledge of movies, or comic books. It's a hobby, why should porn be any different? Let me ask you something detective, over the past twenty years of my life I have been hearing a lot about anti-discrimination. To not judge people based on their lifestyle choices, which *includes* sexual orientation. So if I enjoy say, watching a woman suck off a room full of big black cocks, that makes me a pervert. But if some faggot goes out and actually *does* it, then that's just him expressing his sexuality! How is that fair, huh!? Why am I the pervert!?"

There was the unchecked aggression, the rage that fueled the machine that was Alvin Klug. I knew it was still in there. I surprisingly didn't have an answer for him. Hearing this man talk made my head hurt. Everything that came out of his mouth was awful; depravity soaked in vitriol. His argument was wrong, *he* was wrong, as a person...but I had no rebuttal. Luckily, before my floundering became too apparent, Zel stepped in and picked up the slack.

"You didn't answer our question, what makes you think it was your daughter?"

"Do either of you have kids?"

We both shook our heads.

"Then how could I ever explain it to you in a way you'd understand"

It wasn't a question, he wasn't asking us, he was telling us. Something about the parental bond was indescribable. Even as someone who is not a parent, I understood that there was something...cosmic, about that connection. Something that could never be articulated in a language that we as people could understand. I found that a lot of times this was used as a tool to condescend to people who didn't have children, or to easily dismiss something that they didn't want to take the time to explain. In this case I think it was sincere, there was no way you could explain that kind of revelation to someone. Explain to them how you *knew* without a shadow of a doubt that you had just done a sexual around the world with your own daughter and not realized it. I wanted more than anything in that moment to pity Klug, to feel sorry for him. To be able to feel anything other than disgust and disdain for this lump of flesh and bones. I suddenly felt wrong for saving his life. Suddenly the need to change the subject became almost unbearable.

"The puppet that shot you, who is he? Why did he want you dead?"

"Who is he?" Klug scoffed, as though the knowledge should have been self-evident, "You guys really don't watch porn do you?"

"Not regularly, no"

"He's one of the biggest puppet porn stars around, Johnny Stuff-Ins. He's the one that took my daughter away from me, he's the one that caused all of this. When Heather started seeing him my wife thought I only hated him because he was a puppet, that was obviously part of it, but it was more that. I knew him. I had seen him fuck dozens of girls, and knowing he was going to do that to my little girl was too much for me. I should've said something, I should've known it was only a matter of time

65

before he pulled her into that world."

"There seems to be a lot of things you should have done"

"Do you know where we can find this guy?" Zel asked when he realized I wasn't going to.

"He runs The Stitched Bitches downtown, he generally hangs out there, though after you blew half his face off I doubt he'll just be sitting in his regular booth mucking it up like it was any other night"

"Thank you, we're gonna find this guy"

"Don't thank him Zel," I stood, and when Zel saw I was preparing to leave he did as well. "He doesn't deserve it. I think we've heard enough Mr. Klug, we'll be back to arrest you after you've recuperated"

Zel and I started walking towards the door, I realized I was actually hurrying to it, suddenly not wanting to be breathing the same air as this man.

"There's nothing wrong with me! I'm not sick. My interests never hurt anyone"

"Haven't they?" I threw over my shoulder at him as I opened the door for Zel.

"Murdering my daughter had nothing to do with that!"

His voice was oozing with rage and the frustrations of a man who had spent his entire life trying to justify himself. Trying to explain away the psychosis that had plagued him probably all of his life. I thought about Amanda and how beaten she was, I thought of Colton and all the things he had been shown by his father, how he had been forced to second his father's disgust for what he was watching while still *having* to watch it. I thought of Heather and all of the things she had been put through by this man, before he eventually killed her. I thought about this nuclear family with the 2.5 kids and a dog that had been obliterated. I thought about all of this and stopped in the doorway to look back at him.

"I wasn't talking about that"

I closed the door behind me, leaving Klug alone to the humming of the machines that surrounded his bed and with the shattered memories of a life he never really wanted in the first place.

13

It probably goes without saying, but I had never been to the
Stitched Bitches club. The idea of a puppet gyrating it's scantily clad foam
ass into my lap was never something I felt the need to experience. Zel
however, reluctantly admitted he had been there once for a bachelor party
only a few years ago. Thinking of Zel cutting loose in a strip club and
shoving dollar bills into some Fuzzy's g-string seemed about as feasible as
me doing it myself. I don't know if this made me think more or less of
him, so instead of grappling with the moral quandry I simply watched the
night lights of Los Angeles' downtown whip past me as I followed Zel's
basic directions. Within minutes we had pulled into the parking lot and
were approaching the front doors.

Just outside there was a tall, bald and muscular human male sitting
on a stool behind a podium. Perched on the podium in front of him was his
cell phone on it's side playing what appeared to be old episodes of Happy
Days. As we approached he tapped his screen, pausing on a rather
humorous still of a young Henry Winkler, and turned his attention towards
us. I simply smiled and attempted to make my way past him.

"Wait"

I stopped and turned back to him, he reached into a cubby built
into the back of the podium and pulled out what appeared to be two
business cards. On the front was nothing except the words Stitched
Bitches with a thread coming off the end of the last "S" with a needle
attached to it. He stamped the back of one and handed it to me.

"Ten bucks"

"I thought there was no cover"

"There isn't, the ten bucks is for the card, you need the card to get
in and it's good for life"

I frowned slightly at the odd psuedo-cover charge and fished a ten out of my wallet. Zel also went into his wallet, but instead of pulling out a ten he flashed a slightly weathered and worn version of the same card I was just given. The doorman nodded to Zel and pocketed my ten. We were permitted to walk past into the low lighting of he interior of the club. Once we were through the threshold I turned and looked down at Zel.

"Came here once for a bachelor party huh?"

"Yeah"

"What, you carry that thing with you all the time but never come here?"

"Give me a break Decker, I have a Disneyland Annual pass in my wallet that expired three years ago. Besides, turned out it was useful, didn't it?"

I shrugged as I turned my attention away from Zel and into the bowels of the Stitched Bitches Gentleman's Club. The lights embedded in the ceiling were an obnoxious deep red casting everything in odd gothic tones. In the center of the club was a large stage with two poles on it. Currently there was a Plushie girl topless and on her knees in the center. She was rubbing her hands over her admittedly large breasts while bucking her hips back and forth; INXS' Devil Inside thrummed from the sound system which seemed to be bearing down on us from all directions. The stage was lined with stools for patrons to get a front row seat, and every one of them was filled. There were humans, puppets, high class business men, low class white trash; apparently all men are brothers in arms when it came to oogling the degraded.

"What'll it be?"

I looked down at the voice coming up at me. There was a Beastie girl, a rat, completely nude save for a thong and some pasties holding an empty tray. She was looking up at me with what I would assume was a flirtatious gleam in her eye, but I've always had trouble interpretting any emotion from unmoving hard plastic.

"What kinda scotch you got?"

"What kind do you like, handsome?"

"Laphroaig?"

"You got it; and how about for your friend? You want some muck for yourself?"

"No thanks, never touch it"

She cocked her mouth to the side in obvious disappointment and walked off to our left where the bar was situated. After the brief exchange we walked in the opposite direction of the bar up a couple of steps to a small elevated area near the back where there were some tables. We went to the nearest unoccupied one and sat down. I looked back in the direction of the stage and saw that the Plushie girl was shoving her bare ass into some elderly man's face. He was wearing a suit and throwing twenties onto the stage and I had to assume the latter was the reason he was receiving such special attention. I looked over at Zel who was watching the show as well.

"That do it for you?"

Zel shrugged, "I guess so, I mean, she's attractive enough. I just think the whole scene is a little...grimey"

"I'm with you there, but maybe that's part of it's charm?"

I ended it with a question, but it wasn't really meant to be one. I admit that I have a certain pretension towards places like the Stitched Bitches, but I couldn't deny there was something alluring in the sheer shadiness of the place. It made you feel like you had stepped out of the real world and into some sordid Raymond Chandler novel. Made me feel like I was some private dick instead of your run of the mill police detective; and I was entirely ready to play the part. The waitress was approaching with my drink and as she did I scanned the crowd. I didn't see Johnny anywhere, which I couldn't say was terribly surprising. After the shot I gave him he was probably held up in a motel room of his own with some stripper sewing his face up. I hated to admit it, even to myself, but I took quite a bit of enjoyment in the thought that I had brought that creep's skin flick career to an end when I blew half his head off. Then again, porn had niches and sub-genres of every perverse type, maybe he could start doing specialty movies with deformed puppets. I had no doubt if I busted my cell phone out right now and searched for some, I'd have it within moments. Kind of an ugly thing when you think about it really. The internet is an amazing tool that has all the world's collective information right at your fingertips, but all anyone ever used it for was to watch other people fuck; it's a weird world. Right as the waitress set my drink down in front of me I spotted the VIP table across the room, empty. I pulled out my wallet and proceeded to pay for my drink.

"Where's Johnny tonight? He not coming in?"

The waitress stared at me a moment as my hand hung there in the air, a twenty draped between my fingers. She looked from me to Zel, then back to me. She snatched the bill from my hand.

"Don't know who you mean mister, change?"

I caught her eyes for a moment and though I may have trouble reading puppets, there was no missing the fact that she was lying through her over-sized rodent's teeth. I shook my head slightly and gave her a brief smile.

"You keep it sweetheart"

She turned and left our table as fast as her little paws would take her. I leaned back in my chair and took a sip off my scotch.

"Smooth"

I shot Zel a look out of the corner of my eye, but he wasn't bothering to look at me as he threw his barbs, he was scanning the room looking for other potential sources of information, so I joined him.

Across the way in another small elevated seating area there were more men like the ones lining the stage, each one with a girl sitting next to them chatting them up. At least that was a universal technique; regardless of species. Making the men feel like you were truly interested in them, or that you were somehow more interesting than the pervert sitting next to you was a crucial part of the gig. Guys in places like this, or the Palace for that matter, are paying just as much for you to listen to them as they are to get their rocks off.

"This music is giving me a headache, I'm gonna put some songs in the box, you be alright?"

I looked to Zel, not sure whether to give him a sarcastic remark about being able to take care of myself or beg him not to leave me alone in this puppet haven of sin. I decided just to nod at him. He left his seat and walked off towards the wall to our right that faced the stage. I watched him head off and disappear around a corner, now alone I decided I'd start scanning the crowd looking for anyone that might be willing to cough up any information we could use.

I was just taking another sip from my scotch when my eyes met someone else's. I nearly choked on my drink when she gave me a small wave and started across the floor over to me. Standing six foot five and weighing probably in the three hundreds, the building practically shook with every step she took towards me. She had managed to shove herself into a bright pink bikini, which appeared to be stretched to it's absolute breaking point. Her foamy grey skin reflecting the dense red lights throughout the bar gave her a sickly pink color, from her toes to the end of her trunk. I've said it before and I'll say it again; I hate puppets, but Beasties make me particularly uncomfortable, and this behemoth elephant woman now taking a seat in Zel's vacated chair was no exception.

"Hi beautiful"

"...Hi" I responded, repulsed not only by the physicality of the thing before me, but by it's deep, baritone voice whispering what were no doubt supposed to be seductive words.

"What's a gorgeous little piece of what have you doing in a dump like this place?"

"...oh...ya know...just uh...looking for a little company, I suppose"

"Mmmmhmmm, well baby I think I might just be able to make your dreams come true"

It was like being picked up on by a high school mascot voiced by James Earle Jones, was this what it was going to take? Did I really care about finding a man that shot a scumbag like Klug this badly?

"How bout you and I get a little privacy baby? We'll go into one of these booths here and I can give you a dance that'll make you feel less lonely"

"That sounds...great?"

"Come on sugah!"

With that she grabbed my hand and practically flung me out of my chair. I managed to catch a glimpse of Zel who was now coming back around the corner from the jukebox. He watched me being dragged away, with a look of utter shock on his face, before I was forced into the recesses of the private dance booth. She pushed me ahead of herself because I don't think I would have been able to get around her if she had entered first. I tripped a little at the strength behind the shove and stumbled onto the booth-like padded bench on the far side of the room, which may have been more aptly referred to as a closet.

I sat down and did my best to make myself comfortable, because my instincts told me as soon as this whole ordeal started there wasn't going to be a chance to readjust. The song that had been playing ended and Flowers on the Wall by the Statler Brothers starting coming through the sound system. I had to assume it was Zel's choice because, well who the

Hell else would put this song on in a strip joint? He had unknowingly cranked the surreal nature of the situation I found myself in up to eleven.

"Goddamn it Zel" I whispered to myself.

I took a deep breath and tried to prepare...it wasn't enough. She didn't so much begin dancing as much as merely throw her entire body onto me. My face immediately disappeared between her giant spongy breasts. She jerked back and forth, rubbing them into my face, which some apparently found pleasurable. To me it was like getting a facial massage with very coarse sandpaper. She lept off and grabbed both sides of my face with all the sensuality and finesse of a football tackle.

"You liking that baby?"

"Ohhh" I said, trying to keep the tremor out of my voice, "Sooo much baby!"

"Mmmmhmmm, I knew you would. Why don't we try this?"

Before I could even think to ask what, she jammed her trunk straight down into my crotch. I jerked upright with pain and surprise. She let out a sly chuckle as she worked the tip of her trunk up and down my shaft. I was hoping I'd get hard from the sheer friction, just for the sake of keeping up appearances, but there was no stirring down there what so ever. Soon she was going to catch on that I wasn't enjoying this experience as much as my phenomenal acting may have implied. I had to switch gears.

"So I couldn't help but notice the owner wasn't in tonight, I was hoping I'd be able to talk to him"

The elephant woman laughed uproariously, giving up on kneeding my genitals with her trunk, she turned around to smash her giant ass directly into my lap. I huffed, the wind being knocked from me, but she carried on seemingly unaware.

"Honey, the owner is *never* in here, all he does is sign the checks"

I instantly forgot about my swollen and painful balls and straightened. She seemed to take this as a positive reaction and pushed harder against me groaning.

"What do you mean? I heard Johnny is in here almost every night"

She found this even more hilarious than my initial inquiry, laughing so loud her trunk made an involuntary trumpet sound as she stood and swung around to mount me fully. Her hands made their way up to her chest and she began groping her breasts madly.

"Johnny!? Johnny doesn't run this place, Johnny couldn't run a washing machine. He's just a figurehead baby, a mascot."

I was too engrossed in what she was saying to notice that she had removed her top and was pressing her bare right breast into my face, her nipples flicking across my lips. I ignored the obvious invitation to put it into my mouth and forged ahead.

"Johnny always said he owned the place, if he doesn't than who does?"

"Well, Mr. Grendlewomp of course"

Plushie Palace

14

On the way out of the Stitched Bitches I had the good sense to buy an icy cold bottle of beer, which I instantly shoved down the front of my pants to ease my abused testicles. If Zel had found any of the proceedings humorous (which I had to admit, if the trunk had been on the other dick, I would have) he didn't show it. He pressed on in his typically humorless fashion, which suited me just fine.

"But we already knew that Grendlewomp had sent Johnny to kill Klug didn't we?" Zel asked

"Well we assumed as much, but now I think we can confirm that assumption. Furthermore, this proves that Grendlewomp has his paws in all forms of adult entertainment, which I'd be willing to bet includes..."

"Pornographic films"

"Bingo, thus bridging Plushie Palace and Grendlewomp to Heather and the Klugs. The web is starting to come into focus. Grendlewomp uses Johnny and the adult film industry to lure women in, he does...*something*...then they're puppets with no history; and due to current puppet laws no background check is required, no social security numbers to screw things up, they're just no-strings fodder for the sex business machine. It's essentially human trafficking, or puppet trafficking...or I guess both, technically"

"But what's that *something* he does to them?"

We had reached my car in the side parking lot which the club shared with a nearby gas station. I pulled the bottle from the front of my pants and popped the top on the buckle of my belt. I ruminated on Zel's question as I downed a bigger than average gulp of the beer. Luckily my balls hadn't heated it too much and it was still cold and refreshing. Usually a nice drag on a smoke or a long swallow of beer helped me clear the cobwebs, clarify my thoughts. It was probably all psychosomatic, something I had picked up from too many late night noir films where the hero was always a drinker and a smoker, but it usually did the trick regardless. As I lowered the bottle from my lips I realized my typical moment of clarity wasn't coming, I was stumped.

"How the Hell should I know? I didn't think such a thing was even possible."

"Should we call it a night then?"

"No, no, we can't do that. Candace is sitting on that evidence as a favor, to me. We need to come up with something concrete and we need to come up with it now. She likes me, but that's not gonna be enough if she starts feeling her job could be in jeopardy, not to mention potential criminal charges being brought against her for tampering with evidence. No we need to close this one down *tonight*"

"Any suggestions?"

"I have a plan, but it may be incredibly stupid and it's going to require your help and a lot of luck."

"I'm listening"

"As we drive"

With that I finished the last of my beer and tossed it into the gutter where it smashed into dozens of glittering green shards. As I was climbing in I noticed Zel giving me a disapproving look, which I decided to ignore and continue my descent into my seat behind the wheel. There were more pressing matters at hand than the importance of recycling, if he wanted to, he could give me a ticket. I started the car and we were speeding off into what was undoubtedly going to be one very long night.

The plan hadn't taken very long to explain and there had been a good fifteen minutes of dumbfounded silence before I finally parked the car in the Plushie Palace lot. The entire plan hinged on whether Grendlewomp was here or not. If he wasn't there was very little we could do and it's possible the entire night would be ruined, leaving us with nowhere to go. Luckily the Gods seemed to be smiling on us because I could see through the third story office window that his desk lamp was on. This coupled with the movement of shadows across the glass and the small amount of wall I could see from the car indicated he was there. This is where the plan got a little less subtle, I pointed to the glove compartment. Zel popped it open and inside was a very dear friend of mine, Johnny

Walker.

"This is the part of the plan that seems...ill conceived to me" Zel said, looking down at the bottle contemplating how the rest of the night would unfold. I was hoping he'd grab it for me, but his reluctance forced me to reach across him and snatch the bottle. I twisted it open and covered the mouth with my palm, tipping it over. I then proceeded to apply the booze to the nape of my neck, much like cologne.

"Couldn't you just...*pretend* to be intoxicated?"

"I don't think so. A, I'm not that good of an actor and B, Grendlewomp is clever and I think he'd be able to spot a fake. I have to go full method with this. I need to try to force his hand, and force it in a way that's believable. Make *him* make a move. That's where you step in."

"Right, I get my end of the thing but all of this seems like one Hell of a risk. What if he doesn't react the way you're expecting him to? What if I'm not able to get out?"

"He will, I know the type and as soon as he knows I see smoke he's going to attempt to put out the fire, it'll be instinct. As for you getting out after the show...that's sort of on you buddy. I can't do *everything.*"

I tipped the bottle back and took a slug. When it comes to drinking I'm no amateur and would never claim to be, but a nip here and a nip there was one thing. Downing a long chug of whiskey straight from the bottle was another entirely. Unfortunately I needed to get just smashed enough to be obviously drunk, but not so much that if it came to fisticuffs, or worse a gun fight, that I would be completely useless. My throat was on fire with the sting as it flowed down to my stomach, which I now realized was completely empty. This whole strange case had been so distracting I never even considered eating lunch. That was bad, maybe this whole plan was one giant misstep. I could feel Zel's eyes watching me as I gulped down the first of it and pulled the bottle from my mouth.

"This is highly against department regulations, this could cost us both our badges"

"That's very true" I croaked out, "But so is tampering with evidence, which is what Candace is doing. We're off the grid here, all in order to keep the peace between our respective species on a global scale...this is some weighty shit"

weighty shit? The booze was already starting to take hold. Maybe the scotch at the club and the beer before driving over here wasn't the best idea. Maybe the whole plan was botched from the start. Maybe Zel was right and we should just abandon the whole thing.

"Alright, I'm in" He said

"I should hope so, I already started drinking"

"On one condition"

I stopped the bottle part way to my lips, I looked over to him, my new partner. He reached up and took his doll sized horn rimmed glasses off and looked at me. Maybe it was his intention, or maybe it was just the whiskey doing it's thing and making every action seem more important and monumental than it actually was, but I interpreted the gesture as one of seriousness. It was time for some real talk, and maybe I owed him that much.

"I wanna know"

"Know what?"

"I wanna know why you hate my kind so much"

Damn him. I should have guessed, only a sneaky puppet like him would turn this totally badass, career suicide committing, hard drinking plan against me. He waited till I already had a couple drinks in me before dropping his bullshit condition in my lap, he was *playing* me. That's what I wanted to believe anyways, that's the sort of paranoid rationalization that sober me would have clung to, but I didn't really believe it. Sitting there in the car, a bottle of whiskey in my hand, next to my new partner, about to go into the lion's den with my senses inhibited and at the mercy of fate; it was starting to feel like if things went south this could truly be the night I died. Zel and I were a couple of soldiers in a foxhole just before the final charge at the front lines, a valiant last ditch effort to bring the bad guys down. Maybe it was the booze making me feel that way, maybe it wasn't. If he was asking me this now, in the middle of all of this, he was being sincere. It was important to him to know why. I took one more brief swig of the whiskey and I told him something I had never told anyone before in my life, and I told it to him just the way I'm about to tell it to you.

15

My father, like me, was a cop. He was an honest and hardworking man. He never ascended as high on the ladder as I have, but that didn't really seem to bother him. He was a beat cop. He had always been a beat cop and that was the work he loved. For as long as I can remember he had been a cop, also he'd been a smoker. I guess it was his way of living a dangerous life, always flipping death the bird, till death flipped it right back at him in the form of lung cancer. I like to think that on that day six and a half years ago when he died that Death had greeted him with a carton of Crowley's, a pat on the back and a smile.

"You put up a Hell of a fight there Mr. Decker, but you had to know I was coming sooner rather than later."

Then the two would laugh and walk off together into oblivion. Despite whatever faults he had, I always respected the man.

I remember the smell of burning tobacco like it was just yesterday. It'd be hard to forget considering it was something I had been around since a young age, it'd also be hard to dispute that the reason I myself am a smoker was due large in part to his influence. I had always liked the smell of burning cigarettes, reminded me of dad, and of home. But there was something different about it on that particular morning, me just seven years old sitting at the top of the stairs eavesdropping on what was the argument to end all arguments. As an adult I recognize that it wasn't the smell of his Crowley's burning that was unpleasant, it was what it was tangling with in the air. The smell of pure gin caressed and mingled with the tobacco wafting up the stairs. I was young at the time, as I already said, but no too young to know that most people didn't start "hitting the hard stuff" at noon thirty. My dad certainly never did, so whatever was going on it was a big deal. I scooted my butt down a couple of steps so I could peer through the polished oak bars of the stair's railing down into the living room below. My dad was up and pacing, wearing an old work undershirt and his officer's pants.

Was Dad drinking before he went in to work? I had thought. It was so unlike him, so...tacky and irresponsible. It was almost as if it wasn't my dad pacing through the room taking long, ugly drinks off of the bottle and drags off his cigarette between hurling insults towards the couch.

"It's not *right!*" He'd yell, "It's an abomination, you're spitting in the eye of God!"

That's when my attention turned to where these horrible accusations were being thrown. There, sitting on the couch, the same couch I had spent countless mornings watching He-Man cartoons, was my mother. Next to my mother was an extremely large Beastie puppet I had never seen before. The couch seemed to tip slightly in the puppet's direction due to his considerable size, most bulls are rather big after all. His fur was the color of dark chocolate, his arms were crossed in his lap leaving his hooves dangling on either side. His horns were gigantic, but even from the weak vantage point I had at the top of the stairs, I could tell they were foam. They wouldn't have done much good if the thing decided it had had enough and attempted to gore my father, who was still rattling out horrible derision after horrible derision. I saw tears in my mother's eyes, they were reflecting the light from the lamp that sat in front of her on the coffee table. She was obviously listening to everything my father was saying, and absorbing each blow, taking it in almost as punishment she felt she rightly deserved. The bull looked terrified, but it may have just been that the whites and pupils of his eyes were made of felt, which made them incapable of movement and gave him the constant look of a deer stuck in the headlights.

"Maybe I should go wait in the car", it said

"NO!" My father bellowed, pulling the bottle quickly away from his lips after the shot he had just taken. "You're a part of this too pal! You're all of it, ya know? Fuckin' a man's wife behind his back!"

"Frank" My mother pleaded, "Please, put the bottle down and sit and talk to me"

"Talk!? *TALK!?* Did you try to talk to me? Did you try to discuss how unhappy you were before you decided to take up with this...*thing*!?"

"Of course I did, you just didn't want to hear it. You wanted to play

80

house with your perfect job, your white picket fence and your doting wife. Well I've had it Frank, I've had it. You have no real feelings for me, I'm just another accomplishment, another notch on your belt, another thing to turn to the boys about and say *don't I just have it all?* Whizzleteets *loves* me"

"Is that what you call this?" My father laughed, slurring as he did "Love? Babe, let me tell you something, wiggling and squirming on a fifteen inch foam cock ain't love, it's fleeting!"

"Can you stop being vulgar for a second?"

"*Me* being vulgar, oh that's rich. *I'm* being vulgar by describing the things that *you* did, that makes a whole Hell of a lot of sense. Unless of course you didn't do it, is that what you're saying?"

My mother sat silently, the tears now streaming down her cheeks.

"You're saying you didn't fuck him? You didn't slob all over his dick? You didn't swallow up his glittery load!?"

"ALRIGHT!" My mother screamed in a way I had never heard or thought her capable of. "I did! I did! All you're saying and more, is that what you want to hear? Is that what it all boils down to for you?"

It was my father's turn to be silent, standing slack jawed and swaying with an open bottle in his hand. He just stared blankly, not sure whether to feel vindicated by the confession or disgusted by it.

"It doesn't matter that I was feeling unloved, it doesn't matter that I was unhappy, none of it matters except whether I fucked him or not, well I did, so there. Are you *satisfied* now?"

"...well maybe I am?"

Even at my underdeveloped age I could tell he was lying. I could tell the moment the words left her mouth that he had regretted the implication. He would have been much better off not knowing than now having to live with the tangled web of emotions that this truth left him with. He couldn't admit it though, he was too stubborn, just like he was with those damn cigarettes.

"Good, great" My mother rose from the couch and grabbed her purse from under the table in front of her. "I'll send for my things and have my lawyer contact you in regards to what will be done with Frank Jr."

She started to walk away with Whizzleteets in tow. She was heading for the base of the stairs, undoubtedly on her way up to say goodbye to me somehow. She didn't make it there however, not on her first attempt. She was halted in her tracks by the sound coming from behind her. It started low and rose in timber until it seemed as though the entire house was echoing with it. My father, drunk as a skunk and losing his wife to a goddamn puppet...was laughing. He was just about doubled over himself in absolute hysterics. She stopped dead and began to spin on her heels. It must have been terrifying for her, to have to turn and face the source of that horrible laughter, horrible cause there was no humor in it, horrible because it was dry and wheezing and full of venom.

My father had steadied himself on the mantle of the fireplace, which being in Southern California was more for the aesthetic than actual practicality. He took another sip off his bottle, a long and hard one. Then he leveled his eyes at her.

"Frank!?" Me. He was laughing about me. "You seriously think that anyone would give you so much as visitation rights, let alone *custody!?*"

"And why not?"

"You're a fucking fabric stuffer, a zoophile as far as the courts are concerned. You're leaving me to be with a *non*-human! They're not gonna give you any rights to your son! It would be...an inhospitable environment...and..." He started walking towards her, the bottle clutched in his right hand, which was now extended towards her with it's index finger out in a crooked condemnation. "Even if they *would*...I'm a cop. I have friends in and out of the courtroom beautiful, and I will make sure you never set eyes on your boy again. I'll make sure that if you walk out that door, you're not only walking out on me, you're walking out on him...forever"

She was shaking now, staring vacantly into the eyes of a man she thought she once loved. It was clear now she hadn't, how could she have? This rambling, drunken *thing* in front of her, taking her baby away. She may have been leaving him for a non-human, but there was only one thing standing in that living room lacking humanity that morning. Her tears had stopped, her eyes were damn near dry. She had been hurt beyond crying, beyond such simple things as tears. Her soul had been torn. Her jaw was clenched and that sadness was being filled with something else, something *thicker.* Hatred was coursing through her now, vile and angry. My mother, however, always the more level headed of the two and always able to keep her composure in even the most chaotic of circumstances, merely uttered two words. She wanted to claw his eyes out of his pudgy face. She wanted to sink her teeth into his throat and rip the flesh away letting him bleed out right there on the carpet at her feet. Despite all this, all she could manage were those two words.

"You bastard."

This took all the wind out of my father's sails. I don't exactly know why, maybe there was a special significance to the insult that only they knew, or maybe it was just that she had said it with such honest emotion. Regardless of why however, my father deflated like a popped beach ball. His arms flopped to his side, somehow defeated despite the fact that for all intents and purposes he had won the day. He was keeping the boy away from her and had ruined her in the process. Without another word he turned around and walked back across the room to the couch where his victims had been sitting only moments before and plopped down in a way that only portly men seem capable of doing. He sullenly looked at the bottle in his right hand and the filter of a cigarette between his fingers of the left. It had long finished burning, the cherry undoubtedly dropping somewhere along the carpet making a burn that he wouldn't see for days. Then when he did see it, he would get unreasonably angry about it, cause it would make him feel what he was feeling in this moment all over again. He lazily tossed the butt across the room towards the dormant fireplace and began drinking again.

My mother hadn't moved. She was still in the same place, making the same face at the empty air where he had been. She didn't watch his display of flopping down and tossing butts. It was as if she hadn't realized he moved, merely glaring into the negative space that had once housed her husband. A hoof dropped onto her shoulder, likely meant as a comforting gesture, but his size and clumsiness likely made all subtleties impossible. He leaned his head in next to her's.

"We should probably get going"

She seemed to snap out of her daze and turned towards the voice that had spoken. Just the sight of him made her expression lighten. He was like a release valve of negative energy for her. I didn't realize it then and it's not really until this recounting that I thought of it at all, but...that must be what love looks like. That merely the sight of someone else makes the person feel, just, better. That their presence was enough to make all the bad in the world seem to melt away. Maybe that wouldn't last, maybe it didn't for anyone, but in that moment when their eyes met and my mother actually smiled; she was in love.

She reached up with her hand and touched the left side of his face, pulling it towards her. She kissed the side of his snout and smiled at him again.

"Could you wait in the car for just a minute while I say goodbye to my son?"

I've always found it difficult to read puppet expressions. What they're made of only gave them a certain range of motion, so telling whether one was sad or angry or happy was really a matter of just getting to know that individual puppet. It's one of the things that drives me crazy about them. I couldn't read Wheezleteets' face, I hardly knew him so even attempting to would have been an act of futility, but there was something in the way he pulled away, just enough. The way he nodded and pecked her temple that made me feel like I knew what he was thinking. He was guilty and sad, he felt as though he was ripping this woman away from her son, that he was destroying this family. He also knew though, that when love strikes as strong as this one had that there was no force or emotion that could stop it. Their love was blind to all except each others' light and there was no sense in trying to ignore it. If they had it would likely haunt them for the rest of their lives. He turned then, and walked out the door.

She lingered there for a time, watching where he had been standing in the same fashion she had been watching where my father had been standing, but for the exact opposite reason. She pivoted towards the stairs and made it up three or four of them before she looked up and realized I was sitting there. I had not yet been hurt past the point of tears and my face was slick with them. She halted, perhaps doing her best to process how to continue, now knowing that I had heard at least enough of what had happened downstairs. She composed herself and climbed the remaining steps to where I was sitting. She sat down next to me and for a moment she just...sat with me. No words, no platitudes, no 'you mean everything to me's...just sitting side by side. She finally turned and looked over at me.

"You heard all that?"

"I think so"

"So you know what's going on?"

"Enough. It sucks"

"That does seem to be the word for it"

Again we fell into a comfortable silence. She reached her arm out and put it around my shoulders, pulling me in so she could rest her no doubt weary head on mine. She turned and gave the top of my head a kiss, then rubbed her hand up and down my arm.

"You know I love you right?"

"Yeah...just not as much as that guy"

"No, no, that's not it at all"

"Then why are you leaving?"

"It's a different kind of love Franky. It's no more than the love I have for you, it's just different"

"What about the love you have for Dad?"

"Your dad?" She laughed "I have no love for your dad anymore...he's kind of a dick. Honestly that's more the reason I'm leaving than any love I do or don't have for you or Wheez. Do you understand what I mean?"

"I think so"

She stood now and moved to the step in front of me and sort of knelt down, as if she were in a church pew. She took my hands and looked up into my eyes and I saw that her tears had returned. She gripped my tiny fingers in her's so hard it hurt, but I didn't mind, I just gave her the same sad smile she was giving me.

"Listen Franky, cause this is important, very important" She sniffled a little, brought the cluster of our joined hands to her face to wipe away the tears, I felt their warmness trickle between my fingers. "I love you. No matter what happens. No matter what that man downstairs says to you, don't *ever* let him convince you otherwise. Don't ever believe for a second that I don't love you. My life has always been one big disaster, ever since I ran away from home when I was fifteen. It's been just one big clusterfuck...except for you"

She took one of her hands away from the conglomeration to stroke my cheek, while doing her best to smile up at me.

"I'm sorry I'm not strong enough to stay here, to...burden myself with him to stay with you, I just can't. My life has been one failure after the next and the only thing that will redeem me is if you remember that *I love you*. Please never forget it. Please never disbelieve it cause if that happens, my life is a waste."

With that she leaned in and kissed my forehead before standing up and descending the stairs. I wanted to tell her it was ok. I wanted to tell her that it wasn't that she wasn't strong enough to stay but that she *was* strong enough to leave. I wanted to tell her I'd never forget what she told me. I wanted to tell her a hundred things, a hundred anythings just to stop the damned crying...but I couldn't say anything. All I could do was sit there and watch the only woman in my entire life that I knew without a doubt loved me, walk out of the front door, never to see her again.

The worst part of all of it, worse than losing my family and worse than her leaving is that I forgot. Listening to my father drone on about what a whore she was, about how she left us without so much as a "how do you do" as he'd say. Years of this being drilled into me made me forget. I forgot that my mother loved me for the next twenty five years, making her life a waste without her even knowing it.

16

I was pretty sauced at this point. At first I was just drinking to set the tone for what was about to go down in the Palace, but once I got started explaining everything to Zel I kept drinking for more, conventional reasons. Attempting to stop the flood of emotions I've been trying not to face, to blind myself to the truth of the situation. I had been conditioned to believe that my mother had been the bad guy in the situation, or at the very least that she had been pulled away from us by some puppet Lothario. The truth of the situation was much less dramatic. My mother stopped loving my father for the various reasons that one does, and he couldn't accept the fact.

I lowered the bottle which was about half empty, more than enough to get the job done, but not nearly enough to make me forget everything I had just said. Once the words were out the truth of them kept ringing in my brain and, being my father's son, I didn't want to believe them. My entire world view would be thrown into upheaval if I allowed them to worm their way inside, if I truly reflected on what happened that day.

"You blamed the bull for what happened? That's why you hate puppets?" Zel asked, seeming miles away from where we were both sitting in the front of my car in the parking lot of a whorehouse. I nodded lightly, then shook my head vigorously.

"It's not...just that, ya know? That was just the seed of it. It took years of...sorta...mental propaganda instilled by my father to *really* make me hate you."

Of course I wasn't talking about Zel directly, and I'm sure he knew it. Zel was a pretty stand up guy, the booze was just making my words all jumbled and cloudy. Zel reached over gingerly and took the bottle from my hand and reapplied the cap before depositing it in it's home in the glove compartment. I was looking down at my feet, past the wheel near the pedals, but in my periphery I could see Zel staring out the window contemplatively. He was resting his over-sized head in his palm and in my drunken state I thought it all very funny. Like a giant lime sitting in a fruit cart.

"Thank you for telling me that Decker. I appreciate it."

"Frank"

Zel turned to me, but I refused to turn towards him, the weight of my forehead suddenly seeming like more than my neck could bare.

"Call me Frank, I think we're to that point in our friendship wouldn't you?"

"So we're friends?"

I ignored the question, I wasn't ready to get all mushy and lovey, to change my ways in an instant. He heard me, that was enough for now. I threw my head back as that seemed like the only way I'd be able to move it from where it had been hanging. I banged it on the headrest of my seat and let out a long sigh.

"You drink too much? You still gonna be able to perform?"

"I'll be able" I gurgled. "Just let me get my bearings for a minute"

Which I did. I stuffed all those feelings where they belonged for now, it was time to get to work.

I burst into the lobby of the Plushie Palace with tremendous force, perhaps a little too much force to be believable, but I cut myself some slack on my improvisational skills. I made straight for the elevator until I saw Roxy standing behind the check in counter looking at me like I was a madman. To be fair that's sorta how I felt and what I was going for, so I took it as a compliment. I turned mid-stride and barreled towards the check in desk.

"Roxy!" I roared once I had stepped up to the counter. "What are *you* still doing here!"

She stared up at me looking as though she was bordering on complete panic and terror.

"Grendlewomp told me to stay after to try and bust out some paperwork that had piled up since the incident. Are you drunk?"

"Very!" I screamed again pointing a finger at her. "You shouldn't be here it might be *dangerous*!" With this I swept my arms across the check in desk knocking it's contents to the floor. The fact that the only things sitting there were a small bell and a pen sort of drained the gravitas out of what I thought was a particularly dramatic moment.

"Why are you yelling at me?"

"It's all part of my master plan! If there are security cameras in here and someone is watching they need to think that I'm *furious* and deranged! But, understand I'm not...actually angry with you at all! I actually like you quite a bit, which I wouldn't be saying right now if I wasn't shit faced!"

She laughed a little, unable to help herself. "Ok"

"Well I need to storm into Grendlewomp's office now. You should go home, where you'll be safe!" I headed towards the elevator and pushed the up arrow, then turned back on her pointing an accusatory finger that was merely for show. "You should call me tomorrow...if I'm still alive! We can get dinner! "

She giggled again, though she was clearly worried about what I was doing and what may happen to me. The elevator doors slid open and I stepped inside. They immediately slid back shut. I took a breath and rubbed my hands over my face, partially in a genuine attempt to compose myself but also to cover my mouth so the cameras in the elevator wouldn't see my lips move.

"Alright, once I get up to his desk where he can't see my legs you climb out and find a place to hide, got it?" I was saying this to the very small weight that was hanging on the back of my right leg, underneath my pants. "Oh right you can't respond. Well, that's the plan, hopefully you can hear me alright."

I let my arms drop again to my side, and I could feel myself swaying back and forth and just the slightest sensation of moving upwards thanks to the elevator, my level of inebriation obviously amplifying the effects. It was just then, with the awareness of so much movement that I began to feel sick and thought I was going to vomit. Before I could the elevator jerked to a stop and the doors slid open and I was overtaken with the need to put on the best performance of my life.

I stormed out of the elevator like a hurricane, focused solely on blowing down the doors to Grendlewomp's office and blasting forth like the vengeance of a righteous God. Once I reached the door, which still had it's insufferable Presidential Suite placard on the front, I briefly considered attempting to kick it in. I thought better of it and grabbed both handles and flung them open with all the might I could muster. I heard them crack against the walls on either side and I took a single step in, pointing my finger directly at Grendlewomp who was seated behind his desk glaring at me with a mixture of surprise and fury.

"You shun-ova-bitch!"

Grendlewomp snarled and began to stand up, I realized that wouldn't work at all. If he stood the whole thing would be blown.

"You sit your big furry ass right back down!"

Grendlewomp hesitated for a second, but when he caught a glimpse of the gun holster strapped to me beneath my long tan trench coat, he thought better of it and retook his seat.

"What is the meaning of this Decker?"

"You know God damn well why I'm here!" I slurred, marching towards his desk until I was right on top of it, slamming my palms down hoping that would be enough of a cue for Zel to do his thing. "I'm on to your little scheme!"

As soon as the words left my lips I felt the weight clung to my right leg drop from my pant leg. The rest of it was up to Zel, though I supposed there was still some pressure on me to sell the situation convincingly and to coax the right reaction from Grendlewomp.

"I have no idea what you're talking about, please leave"

"Oh you don't?" I said lightly, "How about the source of your *whores* huh!? What about that!?"

There was a flicker of something in his eyes with this last bit. As drunk as I may have been, I've been a detective a Hell of a lot longer and I knew what that was; he was scared and furthermore, he was about to lie to me.

"I get my women from a number of different locations, all completely legit and above board."

"Oh so you're saying that you don't bring them in via your series of adult video production companies?"

There it was again, quick as a flash through those ebony beads that poked out of his fur ever so slightly.

"Sometimes yes, I'll bring Plushie girls in from my various entrepreneurial vocations. There's nothing wrong with that. It's just a matter of streamlining one's assets. It's good business"

90

"Ah, but what about all of the *human* female stars that seem to go missing from your little productions?"

This time it was more than a flicker, it came in and locked there. He knew I was legitimately onto his nefarious doings, he knew that I knew. His lips curled back to reveal fangs that would have been incredibly intimidating had they not been made of foam rubber. I simply smiled an idiot's grin at him.

"Is this an official inquiry, detective? I'm going to assume from the stench coming off of you and your slurring of every other word that it's not. So I'm going to kindly ask you to leave or I'll call the police"

"The police!?" I laughed uproariously at this, "You're going to call the cops on *me*? Well that's just fine, give em a jingle, I can wait. They'll come in and I'll give them a string of...interesting...nuggets of information, huh? They'll probably be dismissed as drunken ramblings and I'll be reprimanded by my captain...but it'll raise questions, wont it? They'll start asking, what DID happen to those women? Where do you're working girls come from? Is Decker really just drunk and full of shit?"

With this Grendlewomp shot to his feet, and slammed his own paws onto the top of his desk with a frightening force, mirroring my own posture but towering over me by a good six inches. He brought his face in low and bared his teeth. I felt as though I was staring down a cartoon grizzly bear, a very pissed off one.

"You have no evidence of any wrong doings, if you did you'd be here with the whole force, taking me down. But you're not! You're one, sad, drunken cop cliche storming in here like a character out of some shitty Bogart picture. Now I suggest you leave and don't come back unless you're sober and have a warrant for my arrest!"

We stood there for a moment, staring into each others eyes, measuring each others mettle. I couldn't help but smile when I reached the conclusion that mine outweighed his own, maybe it was only by a little, but sometimes a little was enough. I righted myself, as best I could given my condition and attempted to straighten my coat. He was still hunched over, looking more like a real animal than I had ever seen a puppet look before.

"Maybe I'll do that Grendlepoo, maybe I'll do that. First thing in the morning I'd suspect. Maybe I got a little more evidence than you think."

I walked backwards, away from the desk, never taking my bloodshot eyes from his. Making sure he wasn't going to do something profoundly stupid and attack me from behind. I only wanted to rattle him enough, enough to make a mistake, but not enough to do anything foolish. It was an intensely delicate balancing act and being shitfaced wasn't making that any easier. Watching him glower at me, I was pretty sure I had accomplished my mission. So with that I was out of the room and off into the night to meet my partner in crime, who was still sitting patiently in my car three stories below.

17

I rushed through the now empty lobby, at the time thanking God that Roxy had taken my advice and left for the night. In hindsight, I wish I had taken the time to look around, make sure that was actually the case. It may be the biggest regret I have in my professional or personal life.

I hardly remember moving through the parking lot at all, I was a level of drunk that made teleportation possible, and the next thing I *really* remember is plopping back into the driver's seat of my Nova and turning to look at Zel sitting in the seat next to me. I couldn't help myself and began laughing at the sight.

"What?" He asked

"You look like a little stuffed pirate, all you need is a hook on your wrist"

He ignored what I had to say and went back to trying to focus. I was right though, him sitting there with only one eye, one ear and one hand was a pretty humorous sight. Maybe not as funny as I felt it was in my current level of intoxication, but funny enough. I tried to imagine what he was seeing and hearing, half of his senses here and half of them scurrying around in Grendlewomp's office. Popping the pieces off had been easy enough, just like Zel had showed me the day before. It was the taping them together in a way that they would hold long enough for our purposes, but not be permanently adhered to one another that was the real bitch. We sat in silence for several seconds, me slack jawed and staring at him waiting for some sort of update. My impatience won out.

"Did he take the bait?"

"Shh!" Zel hissed at me, "I'm not hearing much, it took him a few minutes to sit back down after you left. You definitely got to him, but whether it was enough for him to slip up remains to be seen."

We sat there longer than I thought we should have been. In my mind's eye Grendlewomp up and walked out of the office right after me, with Zel's hand-ear-eye bug scurrying close behind him, but that wasn't what was happening. I was sitting here in my car, drunk and impatient, watching Zel stare off into space apparently taking in the aesthetics of Grendlewomp's office while the beast sat at his desk jerking off. I was just about to insist on another update, when Zel cut me off.

"He's picking up the phone" He said excitedly.

I straightened in my seat, anxiously waiting for some sort of direction on where to go next, something that was going to lead us to the source of all this madness. I ran a hand over my face a couple times trying to physically push away the drink's influence and mentally sober myself. It was game time now, it was no longer convenient for me to be shit-house drunk, but sheer force of will wasn't gonna be enough. Maybe I hadn't thought this through well enough.

"Hey it's me" Zel said

"Huh?"

"Are you at the studio now?"

"What are you..."

Zel shot me a look and my brain caught up to what was clearly happening in front of me. He was dictating Grendlewomp's half of the conversation. It was kind of weird, it was almost like Zel was a medium channeling the voice of our adversary. I wondered briefly if that's how all mediums functioned, via some sort of wire, but then I realized my mind was wandering and snapped myself back into the present.

"Look I think we may have some police problems." He continued, "Yeah I'm worried. Meet me over at the studio as soon as you can....don't give me excuses, this is what I pay you for! You think you can just get all the pussy and muck you want and then roll over when the shit hits the fan? I built you up, if you screw me now don't think I wont tear you back down again. Good, now get over there, we need to move..."

Zel stopped mid-sentence. I felt like he was messing with me at first, but I should have known better. If not because of the fact that messing with people wasn't really Zel's style, then from the look taking shape on his face. I've seen puppets that are able to lie through their teeth and have not so much as a face twitch. I've seen puppets be told that their entire family had just been killed, and though they vocalize their grief,

94

their faces remain more or less the same. Zel's face now was just as easy to read as any human's. It was overtaken with a combination of things, but the most obvious two were confusion and horror.

"What is it?" I asked uselessly, "damn it Zel move what? What are they saying? What's happening?"

He turned quickly towards me, as though he had completely forgotten I was sitting next to him. Like he had gone somewhere else all together, a place where the things he had just heard weren't possible. Where real was real and this...was somewhere else entirely. On another plane where it couldn't touch the reality of his life.

"He said that they have to move YubbilyToop"

I sat staring at him, frustrated and nearly as confused as he was looking. "Ok...can you tell me what the Hell that is?"

"Only marginally so, I suppose" He sounded miles away, as though he was remembering some repressed memory that he had been trying to hold back, "I never really paid much attention in Sunday school"

"What does *that* mean? Make some sense!"

"Frank, YubbilyToop is a Puppet God."

I had heard the words, but they didn't quite register in my brain in a way that made sense. As I was trying to piece together what he meant by what he had just said, Zel pulled his cell phone out and was thumbing through things on the glowing screen.

"A Puppet...God?"

"Yes"

"That doesn't really clarify things for me"

"YubbilyToop" He began, "A figure in the religious mythology of puppets. YubbilyToop is one of the main six deities of the faith and is generally considered the most important...because he is a creation God, often attributed with the creation of the puppet species"

"You think it's a code word for whatever it is he's using to change people?"

Zel merely stared at his phone, I couldn't tell if he was reading more information on YubbilyToop or if he was just staring off into space, through his phone more than at it, but I guessed it was probably the latter. After what seemed like a very long time, he spoke.

"I hope so"

"What else *could* it be Zel?" I asked, already knowing the answer, or at least the answer that Zel was thinking as he stared blankly down at his phone. I felt like I needed him to say it, like he needed to *admit* that he was actually prescribing to the lunacy running through his mind.

"...it could actually be YubbilyToop"

"God damn it Zel" I yelled, louder and more sternly than I had intended. He turned to me. "A Puppet God!? Seriously? You think that this smut peddler has a religious deity stowed away somewhere that is turning people into puppets!? It's impossible"

"Twenty four hours ago you thought turning people into puppets at all was impossible"

"Yeah but that's different. I mean, people can do all sorts of crazy shit with science now. Hell there are a bunch of Japanese I heard about that say they can clone a Woolly Mammoth! If you said they have some sort of like...Goldblum-Fly-esque teleporter thing that could turn people into puppets...I mean sure, it seems unlikely, but at least it's within the realm of rationality. A *God*? ...a *Puppet* God no less?"

Zel was just looking at me as I ranted and raved. Maybe he had already resigned himself to his belief, but I knew that he knew the reason I was flapping my gums. Why I was rattling off any sort of thing to disprove him of his theory. It was because the idea of it being some sort of supernatural entity, some type of divine creator was too...frightening.

I stopped, locking eyes with his as he stared at me blankly. I had every intention of continuing to tell him how utterly wrong he was, but I found I had nothing else to say on the subject that would make me feel any better.

Zel suddenly straightened in his seat. "Grendlewomp is leaving. I wasn't able to get out, what do we do?"

"We'll wait here till he leaves, I'll go up and shoot out the window to his office and your hand can jump down to us. Then we'll follow Grendlewomp to the studio and end this thing."

"Are you alright to drive Frank?"

"Absolutely not, but I'm doing it anyways. Pull up the address for the studio. We're gonna bust in there and destroy whatever contraption he has that's creating these blasphemies and put him out of business. Feel free to keep your eyes open though. Let me know if you find God"

Zel gave me what I felt was a condescending look as I watched the front door for Grendlewomp, stewing on the conversation Zel and I had just finished, trying my best to figure out the missing piece of this puzzle. Unfortunately I wouldn't have to struggle with it for long, the answer came all too suddenly and all too unpleasantly.

Plushie Palace

18

It was only a short time later that Grendlewomp left, roaring through the parking lot in his expensive looking Oldsmobile. It looked like a model made specifically for humans, but given Grendlewomp's size I'm sure he had no problem handling it. Unfortunately we had to follow through with my plan of shooting out Grendlewomp's office window so Zel's appendage could leap down to us. It wasn't the most subtle move in the world, even in my drunken state I could agree to that, but it was effective none the less. In the time it took us to get back to the car and for me to start the engine, Zel had gotten all of his parts back in the right place.

The studio wasn't difficult to track down. Luckily for us Grendlewomp was attempting to masquerade as a legitimate business man. Maybe some of his business even was honest, as honest as the sex trade can be anyways. Thanks to this the studio was listed among his assets on his taxes and the address is open to public records. As I drove Zel continued to look up more information about the building. Seems it was initially an industrial warehouse, a textile company or some such thing that went out of business. It sat there empty for years until it was purchased by Grendlewomp in the mid-80s at the height of the home video (and therefore pornographic video) boom. He converted the entire warehouse into a filming studio, presumably. To me it seemed like a lot more room than one would need just to shoot skin flicks, but I kept this thought to myself. I didn't need to fan the flames of Zel's mystical boogeyman theory any more. Besides he was a smart guy, if the line between the two was there to be drawn, he'd figure it out without my help.

I thought Zel was probably partly right. Whatever it was that was responsible for changing humans into puppets was being housed in that studio. The warehouse was probably even purchased with that very purpose in mind. Which implied that Grendlewomp had been up to this for a very long time, maybe longer than either of us could comprehend at this point. I tried not to think about the hundreds (or could it be up to thousands?) that Grendlewomp had robbed of their lives, erasing their memories and turning them into something they're not. I tried to focus on the road, I was still far too intoxicated to be driving, so I needed to keep my wits about me and make sure I got us both there in one piece, there was too much riding on it.

The experiences of the past few days and the knowledge that has slowly been creeping in, continued to distract me. I wondered if I'd ever be able to look at the world the same way again. Every time I saw a Plushie on the street, would I be asking myself if they had at some point been human? Did this thing work on animals? Were all Beasties just regular animals that had gone through this "process"? Was it better for them? They gained sentience, which seemed like a big check in the positive column, then again maybe the obliviousness of animals and their lack of understanding about society and right and wrong and mortality was a better way to live. It all seemed like pointless mental meanderings, I'd more than likely never know the answers to these questions, but it's where I found my mind as we pulled up to the curb across the street from Grendlewomp's studio.

"That's the place" Zel said, staring past me out my driver's side window. Then, as if he were reading my mind he added, "Looks kinda big for a porn studio"

I said nothing, but he was right, it was entirely too big. The building we were both examining looked like a giant factory that had fallen into disrepair. The front was made of corrugated steel that had been rusted out from years of poor maintenance. There was a single door that looked almost comical, painted a light baby blue, crammed into the front of the foreboding harsh brown metal surrounding it. I glanced around the parking lot and spotted a few cars, at least we knew someone had decided to show up for the party, I noted that Grendlewomp's Oldsmobile we had seen leaving the Palace wasn't among them. I pulled the gun from my holster and checked the clip.

"You packing incendiary rounds this time?" Zel asked

I felt like giving him shit for asking, even though I had forgotten them earlier the same day, which was why Johnny Stuff-Ins had been allowed to escape. I didn't like loading incendiaries, they made me uncomfortable. While using them it had to be remembered that they were the same ammo that would be used against any *human* perps that happened to show up unexpectedly. The thought of shooting a man in the chest while simultaneously burning them alive was a little too grisly for me. Not to mention the department frowned on it, but they also adopted a "what are you gonna do?" sorta mindset. It made things tricky. I gave Zel a grunt in the affirmative and opened my door, climbing out into the night, ready to do some killing.

As I crossed the street I did my best to case the outside of the building. I saw no signs of security cameras or surveillance equipment, but I thought it best to assume they were there regardless. There wasn't much in the way of cover, so there wasn't really anything to do if they *were* watching, so I simply tried my best to keep my gun out of sight as I made my way towards the little blue front door.

Zel was practically running to keep up with me, but the cool night breeze in my face was sobering and I was finding myself in the zone. We were here against every regulation in the book and anything we did here would be considered a crime in the eyes of the law. As far as I knew we were going to walk into a factory full of criminals that would need to be put down one by one. It was a strange thing to try to prepare yourself for, killing dozens with no official authority backing you up. I ashamedly admit it was a little bit of a rush, but only because I knew even if I had to kill every living thing in this building with fire, it would be completely just. What they did here was a crime not only against man, but against God and nature both. I'd feel no pity for them.

I took the far side of the door and Zel came up to the opposite side next to the knob. We both had our guns out and ready. Looking into his face I wondered if he had to somehow psyche himself up for what was about to happen in the same way I just did, or if it was somehow different for puppets. I didn't think it was, I felt like inside both of us our guts were being twisted with the tension and anxiety of it all. I nodded to him, he nodded back and then tried the doorknob.

It came open immediately and the door swung inward almost silently. We peered around the frame inside, checking to make sure the way was clear before we entered. We stepped in and took in the surroundings. There were a number of sets evenly spread out across the floor and the first thought that ran through my mind was *maybe I was wrong about the building being too big.* Looking at the sets and all they entailed I imagined the building could have been twice as big and not been suspect of anything other than being thorough. We walked straight up the center of the big open room, both of our heads on a swivel trying to be aware of any movement through the shadows.

As far as I could tell the building was split into two parts. The part we were currently in was wide open with sets scattered about, looking like displays in a museum or a waxworks. Each one had a single light on above them illuminating the scene below it. There was a bedroom, a living room, a kitchen; really an entire house worth of rooms simply separated out from one another. I also noticed a couple of oddball ones here and there, the deck of some spaceship that looked just shy of infringing of Star Trek's copyrights, another that appeared to be the interior of a log cabin, just to name a few. As we walked through the displays I got the sensation that the lights on above them, laying each one out in a deliberate tableau, was done for our benefit. I tried to push the thought from my mind, telling myself it merely seemed that the scene was staged because all of these were just that, stages. We made our way towards the end of the room which walled off the second half of the building. The wall stretched from the floor to the ceiling and seemed to be the same corrugated steel that the exterior of the building was made of. It would have simply looked like the back wall of the building if it hadn't been for a single red door in the center of it. It seemed to be made a sturdier stuff than the entrance door had been, which seemed odd. There was a a large painted sign that seemed to be welded to the front of it. It had the words: RESTRICTED AREA. AUTHORIZED PERSONS ONLY emblazoned on it in bold red font. The strangest thing of all though, was that the door was hanging slightly ajar. Through the opening was the only sound I had personally heard since coming in, it sounded like a *whub-whub-whub*, possibly the running of some old and worn out machinery. As we started to approach I whispered over to Zel.

"This is all starting to feel funny, right?"

"Like why would they have a highly restricted area's door hanging open in the middle of the night?"

"Like they're expecting us?"

No sooner had the words left my mouth, there were two audible clicks behind us and a voice echoed out against the walls.

"And just when we were starting to think you two were the dumbest cops we'd ever seen"

Plushie Palace

19

The two thugs that had appeared behind us both held their guns steadily and ready to fire at a moment's notice. The first one, with his gun aimed directly at my head was a man, a human, that I hadn't seen before. As he reached out and took my gun from me I examined his face and it seemed oddly reasonable that this man had turned to a life of crime. He had his head shaved bald, a horribly flat and wide pug nose and a disfiguring scar that sliced across most of his face. He wouldn't have been aesthetically suited for any job outside of organized crime, except maybe a bouncer at a skinhead club. I turned and saw the one aiming his gun at Zel was none other than Johnny Stuff-Ins himself. The side of his face that had been blown out in our last encounter had been pulled down and sewn to the lower half of his head using a tacky day-glow orange thread. He looked like some sort of cartoon Frankenstein abortion. The pulling down of the right side of his hairline to be sewn to the upper half of his jaw had caused the left side of his face to bulge out in a way that even on a puppet seemed stomach turning.

He snatched Zel's gun and tucked it into the waistband of his pants.

"Hey Johnny" I started, "Long time no see, you're looking good"

"Ou chut up KIG!" he attempted to yell through the scraggly uneven crevice that had once been his mouth. "f itwhur up tuh me, I'd shuut Ou 'ere Ou shtand!"

"Sorry? You're gonna have to enunciate a little bit, I can't understand a damn word you're saying" I smiled back at the man that had the gun to me, he wasn't smiling, apparently he didn't find my mockery as amusing as I did. With a swift flick of his wrist gave me a pistol whip across my right eyebrow. I felt the skin split as I dropped to my knees and saw drops of blood dripping out before I was even able to bellow my first obscenity.

"Fuck!"

"Eye cuhrear is OHVER cuz uh Ou Dheckuhr!"

"Enough!" another voice came from in front of us, from where the door had been standing open just a moment ago. Even through I was still looking at the concrete floor watching drop after drop of blood fall from my face and splatter onto the ground, I knew exactly who was talking. I raised my head towards the voice and saw Grendlewomp standing in the door. For the first time since meeting him, he was actually wearing clothes. He still had no shoes, but the rest of him was covered with a black suit, white undershirt and a black tie. He looked as though he was going to a formal banquet or an awards ceremony. For some reason I couldn't quite put my finger on, his fancy outfit filled me with dread. Kneeling where I was on the ground and looking up into his face, the lights from above covered him in shadows except for the white gleaming fangs showing from his smile. I think it was the first time in my life that I'd ever been terrified of a puppet. Despite the intense fear I was feeling inside I did what any self respecting asshole does in such a position.

"Nice outfit Grendle, let me guess, this is the *actual* warehouse where they shot Reservoir Dogs and they threw the suit in with the lease"

I knew something bad was going to happen as soon as I had said it, and despite being very right, I didn't regret it. As soon as I had gotten the smallest chuckle out at my own joke, Mr. Clean standing behind me gave me a swift kick straight to the ribs. I felt the air forced out of me and allowed myself to fall to my side. From where I was laying, through the tears of pain filling my eyes I could see Grendlewomp raise a paw towards his goon. The goon stopped another kick he had ready, mid wind up, and straightened himself behind me.

"There's no need for further violence Terry, Our friend Detective Decker has a penchant for running his mouth, but I have a feeling in a few short moments even *he* will be rendered speechless. Pick him up"

The man named Terry, who had just gifted me with a cracked rib or two reached down and grabbed me under the arms. With a strength that didn't make me feel the least bit better about the situation I found myself in, he was able to lift my dead weight straight up onto my feet. I was as close to face to face with Grendlewomp as it was possible for me to get, which meant I was still forced to look slightly up at him. He merely smiled at me, that horrible fang filled smile that I had learned meant nothing good. He turned away and walked back towards the red door opening it in front of him. He stopped in the doorway and turned back to us.

"If you'll follow me please" He said, as cordial as a viper could.

And help us God, we did.

Grendlewomp crossed through the threshold first, followed by Zel and Johnny while Terry and I brought up the rear. I considered making a move, thinking that the confined space of the doorway may have given me the opportunity I needed to try and overtake them, but there was Zel to think about, not to mention the brute strength Terry had just displayed so nonchalantly. As we were ushered into the large room I was preoccupied with trying to think of a way to free ourselves that I didn't notice the giant thing standing before us. My first indication that there was anything out of the ordinary was when I happened to glance over at Zel's face, and the expression on it said all I needed to know. There was something in this room with us that was...astounding. The type of thing a person sees *maybe* once in a lifetime, something that could literally alter your reality as you knew it. I have to admit I was scared, but I forced my head around to take in what was there, and hope it didn't snap my sanity.

The thing that had been making the *whub-whub-whub* sound I had heard from the other room was not coming from any sort of machinery, it was emanating from a puppet. Without a doubt the largest puppet I had ever laid eyes on. There was another sound coming from it as well, one I had somehow missed while in the other room, though I couldn't explain why I didn't pick up on it. It was just as loud, if not louder than the first sound, a sort of high pitched *yip-yip-yip-yip*. This sound was coming from the thing's second head. Staring up at it I felt my jaw fall away from the rest of my face, hanging there limp and useless. The thing had to be thirty feet in height as the tops of both heads were lightly grazing the ceiling as they swayed back and forth on long, writhing, snake-like necks. There wasn't much in the way of facial features, the heads almost reminded me of the end of large vacuum cleaner hoses. Merely a dark open maw with two bulbous round eyes popped onto the tops of each one. It was almost as if the sounds it was making, were from the thing's breathing. The first *whub-whub-whub* being the intake of breath from the first mouth, the second letting it out with it's high pitched *yip-yip-yip-yip*. It sounded like

107

an exaggerated snoring effect in a bad cartoon.

The thing's necks stretched down to an incredibly large, amorphous body that was covered in pastel yellow fur with lavender polka-dots. There were no other appendages to speak of; no arms, no legs, no genitals. None that I could see anyways. The heads bobbed around, seemingly unaware of it's surroundings, moving with no real rhyme or reason, simply moving around because to be honest, it didn't appear as though it could do much else. The necks bent and twisted wildly and the heads themselves were just along for the ride, endlessly singing their loud, obnoxious, snoring song.

Whub-whub-whub

then

yip-yip-yip-yip

Seemingly without end. I stared up at it, completely forgetting the predicament that Zel and I now found ourselves in, being able to do nothing but marvel at the thing's gaudy beauty. I tried to mentally put together the steps they must have gone through to get the thing inside the building, and found myself stumped. It was so large and the only door aside from the one we'd just been ushered through was a loading bay shutter. The shutter was in itself large, large enough for Grendlewomp to have pulled his car into the warehouse where it was now idling just off to our left, but not nearly enough to have fit the thing that stood before us.

Grendlewomp stepped towards the thing slightly, with his arms stretched out as if he planned to give it a giant bear hug. It became clear he was simply gesturing for dramatic effect as his arms were still hanging there when he turned to address us.

"YubbilyToop...the creation God of Puppish religious myth! You are the only people outside of my organization that have laid eyes on it for hundreds of years. Beautiful isn't it?"

I suppose Grendlewomp's previous prediction had proven true, because I was at a complete loss for words. The things enormity, both physically and through the ramifications of it's very existence were...numbing. I merely gaped at it, trying to think of something smart or witty to say, something that could possibly measure up to the enormity of the situation. I failed miserably and it was Zel who finally broke our combined silence.

"How?" He almost whispered, obviously having just as difficult of a time accepting what was before him as I was. "How did you get this thing? How does it work? What *is* it?"

"It's exactly what you've heard it to be and as I've just referred to it, it's a God. The creation God of our people, quite possibly the origin of our species itself. I don't have all the answers I'm afraid, I don't know where it came from, I don't know how old it is exactly...however I do know it's older than mankind. That it's been on this planet since before Decker's ancestors managed to grow feet and climb out of the primordial ooze that coated the Earth's surface once upon a time. The Grendlewomp bloodline has been responsible for caring for it and protecting it for millennium. I only took charge of it relatively recently, roughly a hundred years before the discovery of this country."

I finally tore my eyes from the thing and locked them on to Grendlewomp. He had been looking at me for this last bit, waiting to watch the blow land when I learned that he himself was older than the country which I had lived in my entire life. Puppets are more or less immortal. They don't get sick, their aging slows exponentially so at a certain point they stop aging entirely. This obviously created an issue with over-population and had caused humans to insist on limits and mandates against puppet reproduction. This was one of the longest running and deepest seeds of resentment between our two species. But what else could the human race do? The only way they really die is at the hands of another, or in a fire or wood chipper accident. Even with this being the case, finding a puppet over a couple of hundred years old is practically unheard of. One Grendlewomp's age, if it was to be believed, was legendary. He grinned at me again, savoring the look of shock on my face, likely savoring it even more because there was no disbelief in it.

"My ancestors rarely used YubbilyToop's gifts. Once per season they would feed it a goat or a sheep as a sacrificial offering. When the goat came out the other side a Beastie, it would be integrated into the tribe and it was believed the society would flourish. When I took charge, on the other hand, I saw the endless possibilities laid before me. This creature practically begs to be used for human trafficking, an unlimited supply of physical slave labor with no messy paper trails. At the time your country was still perfectly fine abusing it's own species for such labors based on their skin colors, so there was no need to use YubbilyToop to make field workers or farm hands...but there has always been a market for the sins of the flesh, or sins of the felt in this case. You humans and your perverse need to stick your dick in anything that moves made the changing of humans and animals into puppets for sex quite a lucrative business. I had an entire gang of raiders that would waylay camps and abduct as many people as they could manage to get away with. Whites, Blacks, Native Americans, men, women, children; it didn't matter. As soon as they came to YubbilyToop they were all fair game. I was able to specialize, I could have made to order sex slaves. Some perverted colonist wants to fuck a small Indian boy? I have five on hand. Some slave owner wants to have sex with his female slaves without the concerns of getting them pregnant? Here's one you can rape to no end, with no chance of offspring cropping up and ruining it."

My attention was fully on Grendlewomp and his posturing now. The initial overwhelming effects of the presence of YubbilyToop had worn off on me, I was now completely enthralled with the horrendous and deplorable history that this monster was divulging. I could hardly accept what I was hearing, but I knew every word of it was true. I doubted none of it, I just didn't *want* it to be true. I was worried that this thing had been responsible for robbing people of their identities, and it turns out it was far worse than I could have imagined. He was stripping people of their lives; pulling them away from their families and loved ones and has been selling them into a life of never ending rape and torture...and he had been doing it for centuries. Up to that point in my life, I didn't think it was possible for me to hate anything as much as I hated Grendlewomp in that moment, I certainly wouldn't have believed I could hate him any *more* than I did standing there. But it was only a few moments later that I was proven wrong yet again and my hate for him would increase ten fold.

Because Grendlewomp had prepared a demonstration.

20

"Terry, Johnny, keep an eye on our guests will you? I have a little surprise for them...you in particular Frank"

Grendlewomp walked over to the back door of his still idling car and opened it. Something rushed out of the back, punching and kicking aggressively against Grendlewomp's chest. I had just finished thinking to myself that whoever it was that was coming, at least they had the balls to try and fight back, then my heart sank and I recognized the person that Grendlewomp was so unceremoniously dragging from the vehicle by their hair. It was Roxy. As he dragged her behind him she continued to kick and struggle against him, but Grendlewomp hardly seemed to notice, in fact the bastard was smiling. I heard Terry and Johnny let out a couple of chuckles behind us. I started to make a move towards Roxy and Grendlewomp when I was given another rather unpleasant crack to the head with the butt of Terry's gun, this time to the back of my skull which momentarily robbed me of my vision and dropped me to my knees.

"Careful Terry, careful...I want to make sure our friend Detective Decker sees *all* of what's about to happen"

I was on my knees hunched over with my face in my hands, trying to will away the pain spiderwebbing it's way across my brain. I felt Terry's meaty fingers grip on to the back of my collar hard and pull me up to a full kneeling position. My vision was blurred, but I could now see Roxy's duct taped mouth and the pleading look in her eyes as Grendlewomp slowly led her over towards YubbilyToop's *whub-whub* head.

"I hadn't planned on adding Roxy to my roster for another few weeks, but after I saw how you two fawned over one another on the security cameras, I knew I needed to speed up to the process...for your sake"

I wanted to jump up to my feet, to roundhouse kick Terry and grab his gun, shooting him before turning the pistol on Johnny and blowing him away. Zel could run in and free Roxy while the villain and I had our final showdown, one on one, trading blows till I managed to shoot the car's gas tank and the entire building went up in an inferno. This wasn't the movies though, and I sure as Hell wasn't Jean-Claude Van Damme. I was just a man, just a cop, and I was starting to think a pretty lousy one at that. All I could do was kneel there with Terry's gun barrel inches from my head as I watched Grendlewomp drag this innocent woman to her fate. I think it was then that Grendlewomp recognized the agony on my face and decided he wanted to twist the knife just a little harder. He pulled the duct tape off of Roxy's mouth so I could hear her scream and beg for her life.

"Frank!" She screamed, loud enough to break glass and my heart, knowing there was nothing I could do. Then something sort of amazing happened. It was terrible and great at the same time, it was something that told me I could have actually loved this woman given the chance. "Frank, listen to me! This isn't your fault, none of this is your fault! Don't worry about what happens to me, it doesn't matter! Just bring this sack of shit down!"

I stared up at the scene unfolding before me, Grendlewomp edging her inch by inch towards the swinging head of YubbilyToop. I got the sensation that the God, or whatever it was, knew it was feeding time because it's *whub-whub* chant had sped up slightly and it's neck movements became more animated. As soon as Roxy started making her proclamations Grendlewomp started pushing her faster, realizing his plans to break me had backfired thanks to the strength of this woman he had underestimated, probably as he had underestimated thousands of others over the centuries. If anything her screams to me had strengthened my resolve. She knew what was at stake, she knew the importance of this entire situation being shut down, even at the cost of herself. I saw that in her eyes and even though there was nothing I could do to save her now, the vengeance that was brought down in her name would be fiery.

All of this happened in less than a minute. There were no dramatic exchanges of *I love yous,* we both knew they wouldn't fit. We hardly knew each other after all and such melodramatics would have felt forced and inorganic. If anything they would have simply satiated some amount of Grendlewomp's hunger for our despair. So after she had finished her cries,

112

after she had bolstered me and reminded me the cost of what was at stake in this room we merely locked eyes with one another. An understanding passed between us. What happened to her, what happened to me or Zel or Terry or Johnny or even Grendlewomp himself was irrelevant. All that mattered was destroying the abomination she had been brought to. It had to end.

All of this didn't make what followed any easier. She continued staring straight into my eyes, not a single tear leaving them as the *whub-whub* head of YubbilyToop came down on top of her. The entire upper half of her body disappeared into it's gaping mouth as it's jaws snapped around her waist. The neck showed a strength I wouldn't have thought it capable of as it swung it's head upwards, Roxy firmly wedged between it's lips, until she was perfectly upside down and her legs smacked the ceiling. With a single loosening of it's lips her legs slipped out of sight. I could see the bulge that was her body sliding down it's neck, like a snake swallowing a rat whole. Once she reached the base of it, the last of her form disappeared into the mass that was YubbilyToop's body. Roxy may have faced her consumption with bravery and without tears, but I wasn't as strong, turning my head from the scene I felt hot streams of them cascade over my face.

"What's the matter Decker?" Grendlewomp chided, making his way across the floor towards where I was still kneeling helplessly. "Don't cry, it's bad for your tough guy image. Besides little Roxy isn't dead and you know it. In just a few moments she's going to be coming out the other side a sexy little Plushie *bitch*. I have to admit I'm a bit curious what she'll look like, I'd imagine she'll become my top earner."

I brought my face back around to him and though there were still streaks of tears standing out on my cheeks, I could practically feel them evaporating off of the heat of my skin, my hatred channeled and red hot. Something told me Grendlewomp felt it, and something told me Grendlewomp was afraid of it. The smile left his lips and I saw something in his face, maybe it wasn't quite fear, but it was enough.

"I can't wait till the boys get here"

The voice was so unexpected that both Grendlewomp and I were confused when we didn't see the other one's mouth move. We had been so entrenched with one another that we had almost forgotten that anyone else was there. We both turned to the source of the sound and we saw Zel smiling and shaking his head slightly.

"The chief in particular" he continued, "I tried to explain to him on the phone exactly what was going on and he thought I'd lost my fluffy little mind, but when he walks in here and sees this thing, how's he going to deny it then?"

Grendlewomp let out a deep laugh as he took a few giant strides over to where my partner was standing, keeping his composure much better than I was if I'm being perfectly honest. Grendlewomp squatted down in front of Zel to get on the same level as him and Zel was still smiling, seemingly enjoying the imaginary play he had visualized in his own head.

"You seriously expect me to believe that you...what? Have reinforcements coming? That you roused the chief in the middle of the night to tell him there was a body snatching conspiracy happening?"

"Frankly I don't give a hoot what you believe, just continue on with your little show here and soon enough you'll hear sirens outside and know that the jig is up and that your entire empire is about to crumble at your feet...I can wait"

Grendlewomp's smile turned slowly into a sneer, he got back up to his feet brusquely and came over to where I was kneeling. He sized me up for a second, trying to gauge my poker face and given the circumstances, it wasn't so great.

"By the expression on your friend's face, I think that's all a load of bullshit"

"He doesn't know about it, I didn't tell him"

We both turned our heads on him again, maybe he hadn't come up with some imaginary scheme, maybe the cavalry was actually coming.

"While he was in your office ranting and raving I called it in. Why wouldn't I? First of all it's protocol and I've always been one to work by the book. Secondly, if I can take you *and* Decker down for his drunken insubordination in one fell swoop, why wouldn't I?"

I turned my head away from him, unable to face the betrayal I was hearing.

"Why would you want Decker taken down, isn't he your partner?"

"Only by force," Zel continued. "He's a bigot and the department needed to clean up his image, so they stuck me with him as his little mascot. Can't be a racist if he has a puppet partner right? Plus he is reckless and just sorta sucks at his job. I call it in, he gets at the very least knocked down to a paper pusher position *and* I become the cop hero that ended a human sex trafficking ring that has spanned for hundreds of years. Seems like everything works out pretty well for me in the end."

Suddenly YubbilyToop's *yip-yip-yip-yip* noises began increasing in both volume and tempo. Everyone looked up at the thing except me, my head was hung low now, feeling how deep the knife had truly been dug into my back. I knew I was right for hating puppets. Self serving cretins the whole lot of them. You have Grendlewomp over here subjugating the entire human race and Zel befriending it just long enough to serve his own needs. The world is truly a shitty place full of shitty people. Grendlewomp looked back at Zel from YubbilyToop.

"Hold that thought, my easy bake oven just went off"

Now I did raise my head, not because I wanted to, but because I needed to. I needed to see the end result, I needed to see what Roxy had become inside that thing. I needed to watch her come out knowing that just moments ago she had been flesh and blood. I needed to witness it, to know the miracle was real.

Grendlewomp approached the *yip-yip-yip-yip* head of YubbilyToop with his arms outstretched, waiting to greet his newest employee, though slave might have been a more fitting title. A lump, much smaller than the one that had been Roxy going down the other neck, began to rise up the *yip-yip* one. It's monotonous cries began coming faster and more labored, it's head flopping around madly on it's neck. To me it looked as though the thing were choking, like a cat bringing up a particularly bad hairball. It then swung it's head downwards and a figure slid out from the opening. A slender figure of foam that seemed to be covered in some sort of lubricant. After the figure a couple of wadded up pieces of cloth tumbled out after it. They were the clothes that Roxy had been wearing when she was eaten. I watched with bated breath as the mound of sticky foam on the ground stirred into motion. Grendlewomp was smiling, wide and proud of his newest acquisition. As she made her way to her feet, there was no denying it had at one time been Roxy.

Even as a puppet, a thing that I had been raised and condition were repugnant and foul, she was the most gorgeous woman I had ever seen. She stood about as tall as Zel at a few feet, but her body was perfectly proportioned. She was nude, since her clothes had come off due to her shrinking size, and she looked bewildered. Her whole body was covered in some sort of slimy goop and her hair was matted with it. She turned and looked at the four of us watching, then turned her head up to Grendlewomp.

"Where am I? *Who* am I? Who are you?"

"Welcome to the world my dear," this left Grendlewomp's throat in a much more intimidating growl than I'm sure he had intended. "I know you must be confused, but all will be made perfectly clear in due time. Those bad men over there were trying to hurt you and I stopped them"

Roxy turned to look at us and I was wounded by the belief in the lie written on her face. Whatever happened inside that thing erased her mind completely, there wasn't even a hint of recognition. I pulled my eyes away from her, unable to bear the beauty there, remembering how she once was. Grendlewomp put a hand against her back and began gently nudging her towards the waiting car.

"Go on ahead and get in the backseat and wait for me, I'll finish dealing with these miscreants and then I'll come help you adjust to this new world."

I watched her go, she slowly walked towards the car, occasionally glancing back not at me, but at all of us. I wanted to call out to her that it was a lie, that I'd never hurt her, that this beast in front of her was the one that had robbed her of...well, of herself. I knew it wouldn't do any good, and accomplish nothing but getting my already throbbing head another crack with the butt of Terry's pistol. The look of uncertainty on her face was too real, everything and everyone was completely foreign to her. She'd have no more reason to believe me than Grendlewomp, or Johnny fuckin' Stuff-Ins for that matter. I turned my attention back to the head honcho, who watched Roxy climb into the backseat of the car before turning back to us with his patented demon's smile.

"Quite a little piece eh? Maybe I'll break her in myself on the way back to the Palace. After I've taken care of you two that is"

I was about lose my cool, start screaming and shouting and cursing, loud enough to bring down the heavens if I could. I didn't care if Terry shot me, or if Johnny shot me, or if either of them shot Zel, the little backstabber. I just wanted Grendlewomp to pay, and if I couldn't make him pay I wanted him to know that the anger, the *hate* that I felt for him was as pure as the driven fuckin' snow, I wanted him to know that if there *is* an afterlife, after he puts a bullet in my brain, I will do anything and everything to cross literal Heaven or Hell, wherever I happen to wind up, to *get him.* I was about to say all of this, I was about lay the Curse of Decker upon his soul and just before I did, a siren started to sound outside.

Plushie Palace

21

The look of sheer, genuine panic that filled Grendlewomp's face was almost enough to make me forget the atrocities I had just witnessed. I wanted to watch him squirm and flutter about like a butterfly pinned to a cork board, but my mind started to wander and two thoughts came almost simultaneously. The first being: *Zel actually did it, he actually called in the team and may have incidentally set in motion a civil war between our two species.* The other one came almost halfway through the other one, cutting the ending off in my mind and filled it with a cloud of bafflement. That thought was: *wait, that's* my *siren.*

All police sirens do sound more or less alike. Mine being a portable job that had been installed into my personal vehicle, it had its own distinct tone and twang. Though it sounded similar to most, it was undeniably *mine,* the same way people knew when it was their car alarm going off in a crowded parking lot.

I turned to Zel who was already looking over at me, anticipating my questioning glance. My face must have looked as confused as I felt because he immediately nodded down to his side, as though that alone would explain everything, and it did. It wasn't until that moment that I noticed Zel's left hand was missing. In the chaos of being snagged and dragged in here, during all of the melodrama that Grendlewomp had been savoring so well, not one of us had noticed his hand drop from his wrist and scurry back the way we had come. I couldn't help but smile at him, despite also feeling guilty for having doubted him.

"You son of a bitch!" I yelled at him, trying not to smirk. "I can't believe you actually called the chief, we're *both* gonna get shit canned for a move like this!"

"It needed to be done, we couldn't take any chances, Grendlewomp

119

needed to be stopped."

"Hey boss, maybe we should get the Hell out of here no?" I heard Terry almost pleading from behind me.

"It's too late" Zel interjected, turning his head towards Grendlewomp who seemed to have composed himself as much as he could knowing that he was going to meet his end in this warehouse, one way or another. "That alarm is just to let you know they're there, flush you out in a panic. If that siren's going they've already got this place surrounded. Unless you want to add murdering cops onto your list of charges I suggest your boys return our weapons, hand over their own and we can at least tell them you cooperated in the end"

The little shit nearly had *me* convinced, and I was in on the plan now. There was no doubt in my mind that Grendlewomp was going to take the bait hook, line and sinker. He had to. He had no other choice. I made my way to my feet and Terry did nothing to stop me, clearly having his own doubts about going down in flames with his employer. We all stood there not speaking for a moment, the sound of the siren echoing from it's place outside. Grendlewomp was mulling over his options, clearly coming to the conclusion he had none. A look of certainty came over him and he looked back to us.

"I've been doing this thing for far too long, It's been my entire life's calling, I built an *empire* off of my familial obligations. I did everything I ever wanted to in this life...except for one"

On this last bit he turned away from us again, looking up at YubbilyToop which was still swinging it's heads around, chirping out it's never ending tune. He took a couple of steps forward, reveling in the sight of it, no doubt recalling all the two had been through over the unfathomable years. Likely saying goodbye, knowing it would be destroyed as soon as he had his cuffs on. I watched, not sad for him in any way mind you, but there was a certain gravity to what was happening. The ending of an era, or several depending on what unit of measure you were using. This thing was and is considered a *God* to these people, whether it actually is one or not I'm still not prepared to say one way or another. He stopped and stood, revering it. Grendlewomp was large and muscular, but his visage was dwarfed when compared to YubbilyToop.

"When I was a child, I would watch my parents bring the sacrifice to it. Watch this holy being *change* things from mere idiotic animals to...cognizant, self-aware creatures. Things with hopes and desires and dreams, some of which I had actually befriended" He turned back to face not me, not Zel, not his goons; but all of us. We were all the same to him now. He had dominion over none of us and we had none over him. That was when I first noticed the hairs on the back of my neck begin to stand up. He slowly walked backwards as he spoke. "Could you imagine that? An animal that I had been feeding oats from my child's paw just a week ago, I was now having deep discussions with about life and death...Heaven and Hell. It was the most magical thing any one in this room has ever seen and I say that with the utmost certainty. I had started to notice, and I'm sure you've all noticed as well, that I didn't look like other puppets. Not quite a Beastie, not quite a Fuzzy. I didn't understand how that could be so I asked my father, what animals did *we* come from. He laughed a little and explained that we didn't. That we were *pure*, sewn by the maker's own hand, he'd say. So I asked him what would happen if one of us went through the sacrifice. He replied simply that there was no way of ever knowing. My father was a man of limited vision because to *me*...the way seemed obvious."

Grendlewomp stopped drifting now, he had come to a stop. I wanted to yell for him to get out of the way, as if he hadn't been aware of what he was doing the entire time. Another part of me, a slightly shameful part, didn't want to say any of those things. A part with a curiosity gnawing at my brain, wanted to see what would happen. It was an incredibly intense sensation and I could hardly imagine that Grendlewomp had been able to restrain himself for what could very well have been thousands of years. Now he was backed into a corner, he had absolutely no reason not to, considering the best he had to look forward to was life in prison, if not the furnace. Zel and I had backed him into that corner not realizing that he had a killer ace up his sleeve, and there was no turning back from it now. Terry and Johnny had relaxed a little and walked around to our sides during the speech, we were all brothers in arms now, Grendlewomp had gone off the reservation. He looked at the line of us standing there and grinned.

"I always wondered what would happen"

As soon as the sentence was finished the *yip-yip-yip-yip* head, the one that had spit out Roxy, shot downwards and took all of Grendlewomp into it's mouth, except for his dangling feet. Unlike with Roxy they weren't kicking or struggling and trying to free themselves. They were simply limp and remained that way as the head tipped back and Grendlewomp slid willingly down it's gullet and into the massive furry body below.

"Jesus Christ!" Terry yelled, having watched his employer swallowed whole.

Zel and I exchanged a look of uncertainty. We had a few seconds before Grendlewomp resurfaced as...well, whatever it was he was going to resurface as. We had to act fast, but how? Do what? Tackle the two guys with us? Wrestle our guns away? Was that the best course of action right now? They didn't cover this kind of shit in the academy. I made a personal decision, get Roxy out of the car and to safety, maybe once this was all over I could put her back through that thing and all of this could have a happy ending. I started to move towards the car. As soon as I did, I heard both Terry and Johnny's guns cock behind me.

"Dun' muhv ashhule!" Johnny yelled as best as he could manage

I turned to look at both of them. "I'm thinking we should get the fuck out of here while we can, right?"

Terry looked hesitantly over at Johnny, "Maybe he's got a point"

Johnny swung his gun around on Terry now, "Weer nuht guing eenywhur wiffou da bohs!"

"Are you kidding me Johnny? He's gone!"

"Sho whut? We jush gho oot ahn ghet arreshtid!?"

I was about to explain to them that the siren was merely a diversion, that if they agreed to just give us the weapons, help us get the girl out of harms way we could forget their involvement in any of this. I would have to, I would have let the two scumbags walk if I could just get Roxy somewhere safe for now until we could figure out exactly how the rest of this was going to play out. Before I could though, YubbilyToop spoke.

WHUB-WHUB-WHUB!

The numbskull twins stopped bickering, I stopped making my way towards the car and in fact took several large steps back away from it. YubbilyToop's *whub-whub-whub* head had been directly above me, I had been so caught up in the moment I had completely disregarded it. I counted myself as lucky that I hadn't been snatched up myself. Then I realized luck had nothing to do with it, it couldn't have snatched me up because there was something incredibly large already making it's way up

122

it's throat.

WHUB-WHUB-WHUB!

The calls from the head were louder and clearly more distressed than it had been in the past. Perhaps it had never been called upon to deposit something of this size. It continued it's screaming and I continued my slow backward steps, back in line with the other three, all of us simply gawking in complete amazement. The thing's screams reached a fever pitch, practically screeching in agony before all sound stopped abruptly. It's neck bulged and the sound of fabric splitting filled the warehouse. Rips could be seen appearing all around as the bulge worked it's way through the neck. Giving up it's spastic throes the neck went limp allowing it's head to drop almost all the way to the floor. It dangled there a few feet from the ground, dead. The bulge finally reached the head proper and it split on all sides, like a blossoming flower, shredding entirely as a giant mass of sticky blue fur dropped to the concrete with a thud.

We all stood dumbly waiting for something to happen, though I'd be willing to bet none of us knew exactly what that something was supposed to be. Then it happened. The mass of blue fur, slick with the same juices that had covered Roxy when she had come out, began to move. Unlike Roxy though the clothes had not slinked off in the process, in fact it seemed that what had come out the other side was larger than Grendlewomp had initially been. The suit hung in tatters, slung over his massive form, reminding me a little morbidly of the Incredible Hulk's shorts after his own transformations. The mass of fur moved, revealing it's shape. Grendlewomp made his way to his knees first, his fists clenched against the ground lifting his weight up. He stayed there a moment with his upper half held up by his extended arms, panting. His breathing was deep and raspy, otherworldly in it's bravado. I think that was the moment that it struck me...that Grendlewomp was *breathing,* something you needed lungs to do. He straightened himself to a full kneeling position, before standing up fully. All of this had been done with his back to us, none of us being able to take in the true horror of his new body, but that was about to change. Johnny started slowly walking forward, like a moth being drawn to a flame. His complete and utter fascination with the proceedings had dulled whatever little sense he had to begin with. As Grendlewomp stood upright, easily twice as tall as he had been, making him nearly twenty feet in stature was enough to make my jaw drop, but the size of him was not what concerned me the most. It was the way he moved, the way his fur shifted across his...skin. He was no longer moving the way a puppet did, there were strong and obvious muscles flexing beneath the matted blue fur. I could see a lighter toned blue *flesh* beneath that fur...and that breathing. Those heaving breaths filling lungs.

"Bosh?" Johnny asked in a near whisper

Grendlewomp turned around fully now towards the sound and what I saw stained my mind for the rest of my days. There was no doubt at this point.

Grendlewomp was *real*.

22

The Grendlebeast's eyes, which had been mere black and immobile beads were now darting from side to side with oily black pupils and shining amber irises. His lips had been pulled back in his labored breathing and revealed a moist purple gum line which no longer housed their comical foam teeth, but long sharp canine fangs that looked as though they could make short work of anything they felt the desire to tear into. His arms were crooked at the elbows and he was looking down at his paws, each finger tipped with a hard black talon that was easily six inches long. The foam pink abdomen that had presented the illusion of musculature was now replaced with the real thing. The shining hard body of a professional wrestler.

Standing before us was a living, breathing, sixteen foot tall monster. I wondered what he remembered, if anything, and thought that either way it did not bode well for my partner and myself. Terry, apparently a much smarter guy than I had given him credit for, was slowly making his way towards the idling car. I think I could have grown to like Terry under different circumstances. He could read the writing on the wall and wasn't too much of a damn fool not to listen to it, and right now the writing said *get the fuck outta dodge*. Johnny however, didn't have the same amount of intelligence, though that didn't come to me as a huge shock. He continued to stand where he had ended up, a mere few feet from where the thing that had once been his employer stood.

"B...bosh?" He whispered again, thinking maybe Grendlewomp hadn't heard him.

The creature looked towards him, having taken a moment to contemplate it's own existence. It's lips were still curled back, revealing it's fangs. Johnny seemed as though he wanted to step back, but couldn't

125

bring himself to do it. Whether the Grendlebeast remembered his life before his change, whether there was some sort of recognition inside of him was something I to this day, do not know or understand. It was entirely possible that in his new form he had accepted a power that he had only dreamed of and anyone and everything in front of him was fair game. He let out a roar I can't properly describe. It was a sound that I imagine a dinosaur like the Tyrannosaur would have let out, and it filled the warehouse, surprising us all with it's fervor.

In a single gesture the Grendlebeast swung one of it's still partially clothed arms down and snatched up Johnny as easily as a child would grab a toy jack off of the ground. Johnny now thought it was time to scream, all pretense of loyalty thrown to the wind, but the scream was horrifyingly brief. As soon as the sound began issuing from him the Grendlebeast brought his other hand around and put his new talons to use. He shredded Johnny, shredded him about as thoroughly as anything can be shredded. Johnny's gun, as well as the one he had taken off of Zel, clattered to the ground at the Grendlebeast's feet with a rain of cotton and fabric. I had never seen a puppet so quickly and thoroughly ended.

That's when Terry made his mistake. Having seen how mercilessly he dispatched Johnny, who had at one point been Grendlewomp's number one enforcer and maybe, partially, his friend; Terry knew there would be no asylum granted to him. Instead of quietly opening the car door and climbing inside stealthily, his fear got the better of him. He let out a small yelp and flung the driver side door open and climbed inside, slamming it behind him. The noise drew the Grendlebeast's attention away from the tattered remains that used to be Johnny Stuff-Ins, puppet porn star extraordinaire, and turned them towards his other fleeing associate. He let out another of those deafening bestial roars and and raced over to the vehicle. I wanted to stop what was about to happen, knowing Roxy was still in there somewhere; naked, confused and afraid. Looking at the size and brutality of the beast bearing down on it now, I knew all I would accomplish was getting my insides ripped out.

Terry punched the car into reverse immediately and slammed into the closed loading bay door, that he had no doubt forgotten about in his panic. The Grendlebeast was on the car in moments. I could tell through the window that Terry was attempting to throw the car's gear, likely with the intention of driving into the approaching monster's ankles. I thought

126

for a moment that it was exactly what I would have done had I found myself in his position and again thought I may have liked the guy a little more than I should have given his criminal inclinations and habit of smacking me in the head with his gun. Before he could do that however the Grendlebeast grabbed the car on either side with both hands and while pivoting his body, hurled the vehicle behind him, back towards the center of the room. I watched the car tumble through the air for what seemed like an incredibly long time. It wasn't until the thing nearly landed that I saw Zel was right under where it was about to crash down.

While I had been standing in a useless stupor, Zel had made for the guns that had fallen during Johnny's demise. I felt like such an ass, staring like some brain dead idiot looking at a math equation on a chalkboard. My simple mind hardly able to wrap my head around the events that were taking place and my partner was throwing himself right into the thick of it, trying to get us weapons so we'd be able to walk away from this surrealistic slaughter. I went to call out for him, but again my partner proved to be slightly quicker than I apparently was in my current state and rolled out of the way back towards me with the weapons in tow. If he had taken just a moment longer to scoop up his quarry, he would have been crushed by the Oldsmobile that came crashing down on it's roof inches behind his heels.

I took a useless step forward, as though me intervening would have accomplished anything in the ensuing madness, but it was an instinct. All I could think was that Roxy was somewhere in that twisted metal, trapped. It teetered for a moment, rocking back and forth on it's roof before stopping. There was movement inside, Terry was attempting to get to his hands and knees, blood running into his face. I glanced through the back window and thought I saw Roxy's face looking out at me, but it was only for a moment, because suddenly the Grendlebeast jumped into the air and landed on the bottom of the car with the full force of it's weight. The roof collapsed immediately, the glass from the windows exploding out in all directions as the bulk of the car's body crunched against the concrete floor. The Grendlebeast jumped again, and again, each jump forcing the metal frame of the car to crinkle in on itself. Then it dropped to it's knees on the bottom side of the car and started slamming it's fists down as hard as it could, over and over, like a small child throwing a tantrum. I noticed blood, obviously coming from Terry's no doubt mangled self, begin slowly creeping out from beneath the wreckage.

"FRANK!"

I turned and Zel was standing off to my right. I didn't know how long he had been standing there screaming my name, but the impression I got was that wasn't the first and only time. I had been frozen by the malevolence on display. I had never been in such an intense crisis like this before, like war, but I had always hoped if and when the moment came that I would have handled myself in a more respectable manner. Zel tossed one of the pistols over to me. I caught it and stared at it for a second, as though he had thrown me some alien technology I had never seen before. I gripped it's handle and felt a bit better, felt more like a cop as opposed to some moron in way over his head. I looked up at the Grendlebeast where he continued smashing what had once been his own very expensive car. Whatever had happened to him inside of YubbilyToop, it had robbed him of the little decency he had. It must have felt my eyes on it, because it stopped it's blind outrage and turned it's head to me. I saw it's face full on, full of raw viciousness. It roared again, shaking the foundation of the warehouse, baring it's horrible ten inch long fangs.

I was trembling. I didn't want to be, I wanted to be cool and collected, like one of the cops you see on prime time TV, maybe say some totally badass quip while taking aim, but I couldn't. Instead of taking aim and staring at him through steely eyes I simply raised the thing in my hand and started firing as quickly as my trigger finger would let me. Luckily the Grendlebeast was a large target so aiming wasn't entirely necessary, I would have had to try to miss him. The first bullet struck and I realized I had wound up with Zel's gun, loaded with incendiary rounds, flames erupting from the hole in it's side where the bullet had landed. The flames caught the Grendlebeast's fur immediately. The next several bullets riddled it's torso, each one a tiny explosion catching any fur in the surrounding area ablaze. The last bullet in the gun, out of luck more than any skill on my part, hit right between it's horrible amber eyes setting it's face on fire.

All of this happened in the span of just a few seconds, it wasn't until this last one that the thing even seemed to react to the barrage of flaming death. It roared again, but this time to be more accurate, it seemed to scream. It reached up to it's flaming face with it's paws, which did no good since the fires from the other shots had already spread to it's extremities. On it's knees on top of the wrecked car it's entire body had

128

become an inferno, it's arms open wide out to either side, howling into the night. I'll never forget the way it looked, arms stretched out like Jesus on the cross, it's entire body consumed by the flames. It's roars slowly wound down to silence and it collapsed onto it's side on the car's underbelly. It didn't take long for the flames to reach the vehicle's exposed gas tank. Despite what lots of people think an ignited gas tank doesn't explode like in the movies, there was no dramatic running away and diving from some hellish explosion, it simply fed the flames to the rest of the car. I stood there watching for a moment; a funeral pyre for three: Grendlewomp, Terry and Roxy. There was no saving her at this point. There was nothing to be done for any of them. I looked down at the depleted gun in my hand as the orange light flickered off of the whole scene.

I was vaguely aware of Zel's hand scampering back into the room from where we had come in, him reaching down with the other hand and reattaching it. At some point the siren had stopped blaring, though I couldn't have told you with any certainty when. He started walking over to me, as I stared blankly at the firearm in my hand. I wasn't having any existential crisis about having taken Grendlewomp's life, or all that had transpired here. Honestly I was still thinking about Roxy, the late Roxy, the one I couldn't save. Even now, in the immediate aftermath I was already trying to convince myself that there was nothing I could have done, but I was having a hard time believing it.

"You alright Frank?"

I didn't answer, I just kept staring, lost in my own mind. I saw him frown out of the corner of my eye and look over at the burning carnage. It had all happened so fast, it seemed like just a few moments ago that we were skulking in here like we were so God damn clever, and now this...four lives ended...just like that. I took a deep breath, the adrenaline finishing it's job, depleting from my veins. My heart slowed to it's normal thrumming and my nerves seemed to sense the immediate danger was over and calmed themselves. I looked up at Zel, who was staring into the fire. His face illuminated in the dancing light. He turned to me and did his best to smile.

"What do you want to do about YubbilyToop?" I asked, almost not caring.

"Well, I think the one mouth being busted the way it is renders it harmless, also if we just turn around and leave I'm assuming the flames will swallow it up with everything else in this dump"

"You know...it might still work"

Zel simply looked at me.

"YubbilyToop I mean, you could take it for one last spin....you could be human Zel"

Zel stared at me for a long moment before turning back to look at the roaring fire. I got the weird sensation that we were standing around a campfire just shooting the breeze, like it was the most natural thing in the world. I tried to embrace this sensation instead of focusing on the fact that there were a total of three people smoldering in the heap and a forth eviscerated just a few feet away . He stared for a moment longer than I thought was entirely comfortable, I almost made my suggestion again, thinking maybe he was as rattled by the whole experience as I was and hadn't processed it. Just before I could, he spoke.

"I'm gonna go ahead and chock it up to the shock of what had just happened here and not get angry or offended by that suggestion. But let me ask you something...why in the world would I want to be human? So I could get sick, grow old, die? So I could get wounded by something as simple as a gunshot? So I wouldn't have my detachable limbs talent that has saved our butts twice tonight? So I could be a part of a species that has spent the entire span of it's existence killing and raping and subjugating? A species that *invented* genocide? So I could count myself among the billions of you that go through your unacceptably short lives hating what you're doing, hating the way the world works and not doing a single blessed thing to change it?"

He looked at the pistol he himself held before tossing it on the ground towards the burning heap. The sound of it clattering on the concrete was loud compared to the crackling of the fire. He shook his head before looking up at me.

"Maybe you're the one that should take it for one last spin"

Then he turned and began walking out of the room. Back out the door, back to my car, back to the real world where God's were firmly held as a relic of faith and monsters didn't exist. I stayed for only a few moments more, stunned just as much by the things Zel had said to me as everything that had occurred throughout the course of this ridiculous case. What he said resonated harder than I had expected them to, maybe harder than he had expected. All the things he said about the human race, what

Klug had done to his family, how I froze up in the face of real danger and may have cost a young girl her life. I thought about all that and all I could thing was one thing.

Damn I hate people.

Plushie Palace

Epilogue

It's been three months since we brought Grendlewomp and his organization down. It was weird keeping something that big from the rest of the department, especially the chief. I've always been a by the books kinda guy, through and through. It's not like me to skew facts and hide evidence, especially in a murder investigation. I'm not stitched together that way. It was surprisingly easy to make things look the way we wanted it to, especially with Frank being so close with Candace. My instinct told me there was something going on there, or maybe something had gone on and it didn't pan out. Then again I could be looking for something that wasn't there. I wanted Frank to find a girl, I get the sense he is incredibly lonely and I think he's still beating himself up for what had happened with Roxy. No matter how many times I ask him, he keeps telling me *he's fine* and that *what's done is done*, but I don't think it's as simple as all that. I think he's the kind of guy that plays off of his emotions and feelings. I think that's what makes him a good cop and a good guy, but I also think that's what makes him kinda cruddy at those things too. Sometimes you need to be clinical about things and I have a feeling that's something Frank isn't comfortable doing. He thinks a good cop thinks with his gut, and maybe he's right to an extent.

After getting Candace to fudge the autopsy report on Bethany, aka Heather Klug, there was really nothing else that needed doing. The entire warehouse burned to the ground the night we were there and...that was that. Terry was a nobody and no one seemed to ever bring his name up and Grendlewomp and Johnny Stuff-ins are both considered missing persons. The most popular opinion being that they had attempted to burn down the studio for the insurance, but something went wrong and they had to get out of town fast. I've also heard a couple of people saying that there was a conspiracy to cover up what had really happened, that Grendlewomp or Johnny had been the one to actually kill Heather and they paid the right cops to hide the facts and took off to the Bahamas or something like that. Crack pot conspiracy theories are fine with me because for one, they can't be proven, and for two, none of them could ever get close enough to what had actually happened to raise any alarms. Even conspiracy theorists weren't *that* crazy.

Alvin Klug was tried and convicted in a surprisingly short amount of time. There was no reason for it not to be I suppose, he had done it after all. His DNA was all over the crime scene, his ex-wife happily testified that he had been a demented man for the majority of their marriage. He was good for it cause he had actually been the one to do the killing and none of the lawyers or the judge had any reason to think otherwise. Al had taken the stand in his own defense and laid out his entire story, including the part about the victim being his daughter in puppet form. The sincerity in which he made these claims practically forced his lawyers to put in a plea for insanity, a plea that was taken up quickly. Al Klug was deemed clinically insane and has since been detained in a mental facility in the hopes of getting him help so he may one day be rehabilitated and reentered into society. That was probably for the best anyhow, I would have felt sorta sorry for him if he had gone to prison. Don't get me wrong, he's a killer and deserves to be punished for what he had done, but he *was* clearly sick in one way or another and I sincerely hope he's able to get the help that he needs.

After the trial I saw Frank talking with the Amanda Klug for quite some time. Smoking cigarettes on the curb in front of the courthouse, both of them laughing and seeming genuinely happy for the company. In fact he told me he's been going out to her place for beers and smokes. I think it'll do them both good. I don't want to get too psychological but Frank needs a mother figure that he never had and Mrs. Klug needs...well, anyone sadly. Anyone that's not some porn obsessed psychopath, anyways. Maybe their bi-weekly visits will help them both in the long run. I hope so.

When all of this started I wasn't too keen on being teamed up with someone that was a known bigot against my kind. Seemed like it would be a tough sell for both of us, but he came around pretty quickly and so did I. Maybe the chief knew that when he put us together, that we'd vibe well together and that our pros and cons would balance each other out nicely. In the end I suppose he was right. I'm glad that he stuck us into the situation and I'm glad he had put us on the case he did. It was an ugly and unpleasant one, but we may not have become the fast friends we did had it not been a case with such high stakes. We became friends because that's what it was gonna take to crack that case, and boy did we crack the heck out of it.

Thinking about all of that; how quickly we came together and how down Frank has been since the night of the fire, I wanted to try and do something nice for him. Show him that I consider him a friend now and not just as a partner forced upon me. I remembered the story he told me that night, when he was drunk behind the wheel of his car; about his mom and her lover. I thought that maybe enough time had passed and his world view had changed enough that a reunion might be just what he needs. I admit I was concerned that it might be crossing a line to throw his mother back into his life as a *present,* but I suppose that was a risk I was willing to take. I wanted to try to improve his life and therefore his state of mind. I think he deserves to be happy.

I was in that mindset when I sat down at my desk that morning and hopped on the computer to try to dig up some information. Even *if* it was crossing a line, I didn't have to go through with it and I figured there was no harm in looking. Poking around I could find almost no record of the woman after her divorce from Frank's father, when she up and disappeared from Frank's life she seemed to up and disappear from the face of the Earth. Then again I didn't know her maiden name so if she had reverted back to that I didn't think I'd have much luck. Then it occurred to me to look for the bull she had left with. It wasn't uncommon these days for women that married puppets to take their name as a surname, since puppets didn't have surnames.

A search of Whizzleteets came up with a result almost immediately. There had been a report issued only a couple of years back, the fact that it was a police report concerned me. That's just what Frank needed, to find out that his mother had left an emotionally abusive relationship with his father just to walk into a physically abusive one with Whizzleteets.

When I opened the report I was slightly stunned. There was the information I needed, as I had suspected she'd taken his name as her surname when they were married. On top of that she was just across town. I could go over, see her and be back before my lunch hour was up; that was if the subject of the report hadn't stopped me in my tracks. There was a picture of Whizzleteets sitting on a park bench with his arm around who I could only presume was Frank's mother...they looked happy. The part that was disarming was the word MISSING in big bold letters above the photo. Frank's mother had reported Whizzleteets missing roughly three years ago. I thought maybe instead of bringing this information directly to Frank, adding more stress to his already burdened shoulders, maybe I should do a little digging on my own. Maybe find out just what had happened to Whizzleteets and Frank's estranged mother.

Decker and Zel will return in

BULLETS FOR BEASTIES

About the Author

Nick Rock was born, raised and lives in Southern California. To go anywhere else would be too far out of his comfort zone. He's always wanted to be a writer in some form, but the book you're holding in your hands **Plushie Palace** is his first legitimate attempt at fictional prose. He describes himself as a slacker, a procrastinator, a writer, a gamer and a pop culture junkie. He spends most of his time at a day job he tolerates or at home with a family he loves which includes his girlfriend Meghan and their four cats Biz, Boba, Pumpkin and Clover. He is usually either video/board gaming or reading comic books. He has an *extensive* X-men collection, you should see it some time.